# The
# Sod Turners

# The
# Sod Turners

## Katherine Marko

### Illustrated by Harry Kane

**Criterion Books**
New York

*To my husband, Alex,*
*our daughter, Monica,*
*and our sons, John and Joel*

# Contents

## Chapter One

# Home in Kansas

The bright August sun was shining on the stretch of Kansas prairie south of the little town of Wellington. Desty Shawn could feel its heat, soaked up by the dust of the road, on her bare feet. Its rays burned through the shoulders of her faded calico dress and the top of her sunbonnet. She could see its gleam in the coppery braids of Fiddle, her ten-year-old twin sister, who was skipping happily ahead of her.

But Desty wasn't happy. She felt like crying.

Fiddle stopped and waited impatiently for her to catch up. "You sure are pokey this morning."

As usual, Fiddle's sunbonnet strings were still tied at her throat, but the bonnet was pushed back so that it hung limply on her shoulders. She and Desty were on their way home from the general store on the edge of town.

Fiddle shifted the small grocery basket from her left arm to her right, and started off again, calling, "Hurry up!"

But Desty had no wish to hurry. She wanted to think. The news they had heard at the store might change her whole life.

There were always several oldtimers at the store, sitting near the big round stove and the pickle barrel. They usually smoked and played checkers quietly, not saying very much. But today, they were all talking at once to the two townsmen who brought the news. Everyone was excited. There was to be a land rush into the Cherokee Strip!

The Cherokee Strip was a piece of land about fifty-eight miles wide and one hundred sixty-five miles long. It ran along the southern border of Kansas in the Indian territory called Oklahoma. It had belonged to the Indians who rented it to cattlemen for grazing land, but that was all finished now. The government in Washington was opening it for settlement, just like other parts of Oklahoma.

"Just what we've been waiting for," one of the townsmen said, as he wrote the date of the land rush in big, bold numbers on the gray slate hanging on the wall: **SEPTEMBER 16, 1893.**

"That's next month," Fiddle had said, her eyes sparkling as if the whole land rush would be hers alone.

There had been other Runs, as land rushes were called,

into different sections of the Indian territory. Desty had heard a great deal of talk about them. But she knew her father would definitely want to be in this one. Papa had often said if there were ever another land rush, he would go. And then he would take the whole family, Mama and Fiddle and her, and their two older brothers, Burt, fifteen and Jason, thirteen. That meant moving away from here and she did not want to move away.

Fiddle stopped again. She was teetering back and forth, making the basket bump against her legs. She handed it to Desty. "Here, it's your turn to carry it."

In the basket lay a couple of small packages: some sugar, a can of baking powder, a spool of thread and tobacco for Papa's pipe. They were always going to the store it seemed, because they could never buy much at a time. Mama said money never stretched far enough.

But Desty never minded going often to the store. She and Fiddle talked and planned and dreamed as they walked along. And always they saw Marietta Hobson, their dearest friend. Marietta had light gold hair which always hung in perfect long curls — never in braids like hers and Fiddle's. Mama only put their hair up in curls for special occasions, like Christmas and birthdays. And Marietta had a dog, too, a perky little terrior named Bouncey.

They were passing Marietta's house, which stood sparkling white in the middle of a small pine grove on the east side of the road. It was just halfway between their house and the store, and they always stopped at her pump for a drink of water on the way *to* the store. Coming home, they were supposed to pass on by.

"I'm thirsty," Fiddle said, putting her hands on the white picket fence.

Desty reminded her: "Mama said it's not polite to stop in again."

Fiddle seemed to forget her thirst quickly. She started to skip once more. "Wouldn't it be wonderful if Papa built us a house in the Strip just like the one we were born in?"

They never tired of having Mama tell them about *that* house and how they were named. They were born on Christmas Eve. The family lived in Ohio then. Mama heard the carolers outside singing Adeste Fidelis. She named one of them Adeste Marie, and the other, Mary Fidelis. With two older brothers like Burt and Jason, those names were soon changed to Desty and Fiddle.

And Mama described the house so beautifully. It was painted white and it had a porch, a big lawn and a garden. Outside the kitchen door, there was a trellis of rambling roses on one side and on the other, a honeysuckle that made the whole dooryard smell sweet.

They had moved three times since then: to Illinois, to Missouri, then down here to Kansas. The last time was the only one Desty remembered clearly. She was too little then to care much. But now she did care.

Papa had fixed up the house they lived in now. Best of all was the little bedroom she and Fiddle shared. Mama had painted it a soft pale green, the color of the willows alongside the pond. She would hate to leave that little room.

She tried hard to think of other things, like soft baby chicks or her Sunday shoes with shiny white buttons. But she could not forget the excited voices of the men in the store. "Land rush . . . good land . . . free land . . . homestead . . . good land . . . Cherokee Strip!"

"What's so much better about the Strip than this land," she said half-aloud, as she looked around at the grassy acres on either side of her. Farther on, stretches of wire fenced in fields of corn, potatoes, or maybe pasture land. Some of them were Papa's fields. She could always wander to any patch of wildflowers and pick them for Mama. Or wild strawberries in season; or nuts in the fall.

Fiddle looked at her. "What did you say? I couldn't hear you."

Desty repeated what she said and added: "And there might not be any roads in the Strip either." She stared ahead at the rutted old road that rambled straight south past their house to the border of the Indian territory. The coarse grass, grayed by a coating of dust, grew up along the edge and sprang high in the center between the wagon tracks.

"Papa doesn't own our farm," Fiddle said. "Papa wants to own his own land."

Yes, that was true, Papa only rented the place they lived on now.

Desty stooped to pick a few daisies. Their petals looked so forlorn and droopy from the hot, dry air, she hoped it would rain. All the cornfields held stunted stalks instead of tall green ones.

Fiddle read her thoughts. "Papa said if we don't have rain soon, the crops won't amount to much."

But what did it matter if they were going to move away anyway?

Fiddle went on skipping and prancing, with her braids bouncing this way and that. Suddenly she stopped, put her hands on her hips and leaned her head to one side. "Aren't you excited, Desty, even a little bit?"

Desty shook her head. "I wish the government would change its mind about giving the land away. Or make folks pay so much for it, they couldn't buy any. Or that the Indians would come charging back and claim it for themselves again." She said it all in a rush, and then she thought of Papa and felt guilty.

Fiddle caught her arm. "If Papa decides to go, we'll be in a real land rush like Uncle Gus used to tell us about. Remember?"

"Yes, I remember," Desty answered. Uncle Gus was not really their uncle but an old neighbor who was in the 1889 Run into the Oklahoma territory, just four years ago. He could not file a claim because the quarter-section he had chosen was contested by three other men. He was one of the losers. But he was forever ready to tell of how thrilling the land rush was. She and Fiddle and Burt and Jason were his most willing listeners, except sometimes when Uncle Gus used swear words.

Then Mama would shoo them out to play, saying they were too young to hear "strong talk."

But Papa always listened, and said if he had not been sick at that time he would have been in that Run himself.

That was true. Papa had brought the family from Missouri, heading for the territory when he fell sick and could not go farther. But he never stopped wishing and hoping. He and Uncle Gus resolved that if there were ever another land rush, they both would be in it. Uncle Gus even went down to the Cherokee Strip and drew maps of places where he thought the best homesteading claims would be. He and Papa often studied those maps.

But last year, Uncle Gus had moved to his nephew's place in California.

Fiddle started to walk backward, now, in front of Desty so she could face her. "I'm so excited, I could burst," Fiddle said, sounding awfully happy.

But Desty still felt all mixed-up and sad. "I don't care, I don't want to go," she said.

Fiddle stopped. "Why?"

"Because we'll have to leave Marietta behind and we never had a better friend than her." She could not explain to Fiddle all her other feelings about not wanting to leave.

Fiddle did not sound the least bit worried. "We'll make new friends and we can write to Marietta. We all write good enough to write a letter — don't we?" Fiddle's writing was usually difficult to understand, but Desty's was much better. She liked school. That was another thing. There might not be a school in the Strip for a long, long time.

"I don't care — I don't want to move away." That was all she could say.

Fiddle fell into step beside her and reached out her hand. "I'll carry the basket again."

It was just midmorning, but the day was already sultry. A few grasshoppers jumped lazily out of their way, and Desty heard a frog croak a few times as if he had just awakened. She guessed he was at the little pond. It lay alongside the road just up ahead. Twice they had to stand aside as a wagon lurched past them. The first was driven by a neighboring farmer, a friend of their family. He gave them a quick wave. The second driver did not bother; he was a stranger.

Desty wished she could be anxious for adventure, like

Fiddle. Fiddle's eyes were still sparkling and a smile touched the corners of her mouth. It was strange how different they were. She had hazel eyes like Fiddle's, white even teeth, a short nose with probably the same number of freckles sprinkled across its bridge. They looked as much alike as any other twin sisters would, yet they were altogether different.

Fiddle, as Papa often said, was named right. She could say "Fiddle-dee-dee" to almost anything and the next moment be waiting for something new to happen. But Desty could not feel like that. Papa said she was like Mama, quiet and settled.

As they neared the pond, the frog croaked again. He was hiding near the edge, most likely. It was only a small pond, just a hollow filled mostly by rain, but it never dried up entirely because it had an underground spring. During this dry spell it had shrunk more than usual, but you could cool off quicker than a wink, just by standing in it. It nestled in a spot of low land only a stone's throw from the road.

She and Fiddle stopped by now, as they always did, unless Mama strictly told them to hurry. They drew their skirts and petticoats up to their knees and went wading. That was the best part of going barefoot — no shoes and stockings to bother with.

On the far side stood her favorite trees, two big willows that dipped their branches down until their narrow bladelike leaves dragged in the water. Between them grew a few small haw bushes, gray now, like the grass, with dust that sifted down from the road.

The water around the rim of the pool was warm from the sun. Desty could feel it growing cooler and cooler as she stepped towards the middle. There, the ice-cold water sent shivers up her legs and she knew she was right over the spring. She closed her eyes as the delicious coolness spread all the way up to the top of her head.

If she had to go homesteading, she hoped there would be ponds like this in the Strip. Some days when they went wading, they caught polywogs, and some days they brought a bag of lunch to picnic under the willows. When the water froze in the winter, they skated on it.

Another wagon and team rumbled by, going south. She did not try to see who it was.

Fiddle went splashing back towards the bank. "Come on, let's see if Mama heard the news yet." Other days Fiddle almost had to be dragged out of the water.

Desty followed, but she had a feeling that the news would reach their house before they would. She could see their wet footmarks dark against the cracked dry mud where the water had receded. She began to grow awfully warm again as she dragged her feet through the grass to dry them.

"Stop daydreaming and come on," Fiddle called.

"There's time," she answered. Somehow she felt Mama would not like the news.

# Chapter Two

## "Are we going?"

Fiddle ran on ahead, but Desty did not try to catch up with her now. Everything they passed seemed to have much more importance than usual, like the clumps of sunflowers with such large heads that they hung over from their own weight.

Even their house looked different to her now. She could see it from a distance since it stood out in the open, facing west, sunwashed and windswept. It seemed much dearer to her, with its weathered clapboards and built-on rooms that the owner allowed Papa to add. And the old back porch on which Mama kept the wooden tubs and copper boiler for washing.

Moving away would not be so bad if you could pack

up the whole house and garden and friends and every-thing you treasured and take them along like clothes or dolls.

Papa was not working in the field on the north side of the house where he had been when they left for the store. He must have heard the news. Anyone going by on the road would have passed the word.

Fiddle was waiting at the picket fence out front. "You're so pokey today," she said again.

Going around to the back they heard a stomping sound coming from the barn. Desty knew without looking that Papa was getting Champ ready to go into town. But she glanced back just as Papa came out of the barn with his saddle. Papa's back was badly hurt when he was thrown from a horse as a young man. Therefore he could not ride hard or long, but he often rode the short distance to town, if he did not want to take the time to harness the horses to the buckboard or wagon.

Papa was usually calm and easy-going, working with slow, sure movements. But now his hands were quick and deft, and, with each jerk of the cinch strap, he tossed his thick black hair. And all the while he was whistling "Blue Tail Fly."

Fiddle was fidgeting on the door step. "Come on, Mama's waiting for the sugar."

"Well, why don't you go on in and give it to her," Desty snapped. She saw Fiddle look at her oddly because she seldom spoke that sharply to anyone, but she could not help it. Then she felt sorry and went inside with Fiddle.

The kitchen was stifling from the oven, but it was full of that wonderful smell of fresh bread. Mama was sifting

flour into a heavy crockery bowl, and she did not look up when they came in, as she usually did.

"There's going to be a land rush," Fiddle blurted out.

Mama did not answer. She just reached for the sugar sack and measured some into a smaller bowl. Desty could tell she was discouraged and sad. She was too silent. And her long slender hands looked as though they were tired as she slowly stirred the wooden spoon around the bowl. Mama was a tall woman but she looked stooped now.

Fiddle stood looking out of the window for a minute. "What's wrong, Mama?"

Mama still did not look up from her task. It seemed she bent her head a little lower. "Why nothing, Fiddle, nothing yet."

"What do you mean — nothing yet?"

"Nothing at all is wrong," Mama repeated. "Now run out to the hen coop and see if there are any eggs so I can get on with this cake."

Desty followed Fiddle through the door. She tried to tell herself that Mama might be worried about Aunt Bessie, Mama's younger sister. Goodness, Desty thought, she had almost forgotten about Aunt Bessie since she heard the news in the store. But she knew that was not the reason Mama was worried.

Aunt Bessie had lived with Mama and Papa and the family ever since they moved to Kansas. And just last week she had married Luke Andrews. She almost seemed like an older sister to Desty, but now she would be going to live on Luke's farm with his parents after she came back from her honeymoon.

Desty would miss seeing her every day, but it would

be much worse moving far away from her. Aunt Bessie was a quiet young woman, so quiet that some folks thought her timid. But it was just her gentleness. When she reached out to pat someone's hand, she did not have to speak. Her soft blue eyes always looked as though she knew exactly how that person felt.

On the way to the hen coop, Desty saw Papa going toward the house, his long thin legs taking quick strides.

"Oh, I'm going to ask Papa if we're going to be in the land rush," Fiddle began, and would have run to him, but Desty grabbed her arm.

"No, not yet."

"Stop, you'll tear my sleeve," Fiddle shouted. Desty let go. Fiddle already had one tear in her skirt which all of Mama's skillful stitches could not hide. And the little garnet sprigs of color were hardly recognizable on the brown calico where Fiddle had gotten some walnut stains.

Fiddle's voice was angry and squeaky. "Why shouldn't I ask Papa?"

"Just because."

They found seven eggs and again Fiddle was ready to rush back to the house to question Papa. But Desty did not want to hear the final word yet.

When they reached the porch step, she motioned Fiddle to sit down with her. "You don't have to find out right now anyhow. Mama and Papa are talking."

They were taught not to eavesdrop, but their parents' voices came out the door. Papa's was excited as it always was when he was eager to start on something new. "But, Nell, we can make a new start. This land here isn't much good anyhow. We can have —"

"But someday we might be able to buy this place. This land is as good as any around here. This dry spell stunted crops all over. It wasn't the land that did it." Mama's voice was high, weary and worried. "Besides, Henry," (Mama always called Papa by his full Christian name, not "Hank" like other folks did) "didn't you want to stay near a town so that it would be easier to find work to tide us over when things go badly?"

Papa did not lose any of his enthusiasm. "But Nell, I'll build you a nice new home. There'll be a new town springing up and I'll rent a place and start a livery stable. We'll have land, a home, and a business!"

Desty knew Papa's white teeth would be flashing in a coaxing smile now, and he would run his calloused hand through his bushy, black hair. And in his eyes would be a sparkle that made his whole face shine.

"But forever on the move is not good for the children," Mama answered. Desty remembered how Mama would gently scold Papa when he would joke about having itchy feet, unable to stay in one place very long.

"In the last Run," Mama went on, "all those poor folks who couldn't make a go of it had to give up. Some of them had no place to go back to, they spent all their money and used up all their food. I can remember so well all those who passed here —"

"Now, now, Nell, you worry too much. That won't happen to us," Papa assured her.

"Well, perhaps," Mama said quietly, "if you make one promise, Henry. . . ." Her next words were lower and Desty could not hear what was said. Yet she had a feeling that Mama would be wearing that slow, tender smile that did not seem to fit any other face as well as Mama's, and her eyes would be soft because she could not deny Papa anything.

Then, Desty guessed, Mama would smooth her chestnut brown hair back and go on mixing the cake. Mama's hair was getting a little gray lately, but it still lay in soft waves just above her forehead.

"The eggs." Fiddle was jiggling her arm. "Mama's waiting for them."

Then Fiddle stumbled through the door. "Are we going?" she asked, before she scarcely had regained her balance.

"We'll see, Fiddle, we'll see," Papa said patting her head.

Fiddle clapped her hands. "Then we'll be sodbusters. That's what Uncle Gus always called them."

"I don't like that name," Desty said.

Then Papa patted her head. "Oh, it just means people who turn the sod with their plows."

"Well, then why can't we be called 'sod turners'?"

Papa grinned at her. "No reason why we couldn't be," he said.

Just then the boys came hurrying in. Papa put his hands on his hips and made a stern face. "Aren't you boys supposed to be cutting down some dead trees near the meadow?" He tousled their hair with his large-knuckled hands.

Burt quickly smoothed his hair, which was thick and black like Papa's. He did not seem to like it ruffled up. Burt was always quiet. He listened more than he talked, but Desty noticed that since he had turned fifteen, he was trying to act grown-up. He became angry more often

now when she and Fiddle teased him. She could understand Jason much better. Jason always laughed and
teased right back at her and Fiddle.

Jason's curly hair was the same coppery color as hers
and always looked tousled anyway. He ducked away
from Papa now, and held up his hand, laughing. "Know
what we heard? The land rush is going through."

Papa laughed with him. "Oh, you heard?"

Burt, still sober-faced explained. "A rider stopped at
the lower field. He told us."

"Yeah," Jason began again. "Just think. A hundred
and sixty acres free —"

Mama interrupted him. "I think that's enough land
rush talk for today."

Papa took his tobacco and went outside with the boys.

Mama was smiling now, and her words were light and
cheerful. "You girls grease these cake pans for me."

Desty wondered what Mama had asked Papa to promise. He must have said "yes."

# Chapter
## Three
# *Papa's Promise*

Usually, Desty could fall asleep as soon as she went to bed, but that night she could not. She knew Fiddle was sleeping, because she could hear her breathing deeply and evenly. She wished Fiddle were awake too, so that she could ask her if she had any idea why Mama agreed so quickly to go homesteading in the Cherokee Strip.

However, when she awoke next morning, she realized she must have slept pretty soundly after all. The early sun was bright and the air was full of bird songs. At their little window, the muslin curtains were puffing into the room and falling softly on the window sill again; puffing and falling, in the light warm breeze. She could feel it on her bare arms as they lay on top of her coverlet.

Stretching and yawning, she sat up. At the back of her

mind, she had a feeling that she was forgetting something important. Then she remembered — the land rush! The sunshine did not seem so bright anymore. She leaned back on her pillow and let her eyes scan the little room. Her look rested on the picture, "The Stable at Bethlehem," on the wall at the chimney corner; then on the bureau in which she and Fiddle kept their clothes and treasures. Over in the corner stood the cane-seated chair that was always piled high with whatever Fiddle happened to bring upstairs.

Then she looked at Fiddle as she stirred in her sleep. Fiddle's face wore a little smile as though she were having a pleasant dream.

Desty got up, said her morning prayers and dressed very quietly. She tried to think of something that would make her happy. What could she think of? Books? She loved books, but she did not have many. Thinking about school could not make her happy now either. And again she worried about the new territory not having a school for a long, long time.

How could she learn more than she knew now? Papa always said she liked to *learn* new things, and that Fiddle liked to *try* new things.

Oh, there would *have* to be a school! She often heard Mama say, "Education is something that no one can take away from you. Whatever education you get is yours forever." Surely then, Mama would not want them to stop going to school.

She was about to tiptoe downstairs, when Fiddle awoke and almost shouted: "Good morning."

"Oh, good morning." She knew why Fiddle greeted her. Fiddle was not always that thoughtful. Most of the

time, she just jumped out of bed and tried to beat Desty
getting dressed and ready for breakfast. But this morning
Desty knew she was remembering the land rush, and her
excitement would be just as high and wild as it was yesterday. Desty did not like that, because she wanted to
forget about the Cherokee Strip as long as possible.

Fiddle gave herself a little hug. "It's early yet. Let's
pack some of our things before we go downstairs. I just
can't wait."

Never before had Desty felt like slapping Fiddle, but
now she felt that way. But that would not be right. Fiddle
was not to blame for anything that was happening, she
was only enjoying it.

Desty started down the stairs. "No, I just don't want
to get anything ready yet."

"Why?"

"Because." She wondered if Fiddle would ever stop
asking "why" and if she herself would ever find a better
answer than "because."

Then Fiddle raced past her down the stairs and she
followed, measuring her steps as though she were count-
ing them.

"Mmm, oatmeal," Fiddle crooned, as she sat down at
the table and slapped her napkin onto her lap. Mama
was very strict about napkins.

"We have oatmeal every morning," Desty said. She
wished Fiddle would stop being so overly happy about
every little thing that she never bothered noticing before.

Breakfast went fast that morning. No one ever really
dawdled over breakfast, but that day it went too quickly,
she thought. Maybe it was because she was trying to slow
up everything in her own mind.

Then Mama told them the big reason for hurrying this

morning. Aunt Bessie and Luke — he was their *Uncle Luke* now — had come home the night before from their honeymoon.

"They're coming for supper," Mama said brightly. "So you girls get everything dusted well after you make the beds."

Papa was still loitering about the kitchen. He had taken care of Champ, and Star, their older work horse, and the cow. But he usually would have left by now for field work or whatever had to be done outdoors. Desty guessed he would not be doing much around the land anymore if they were going to leave it.

"I'll kill three chickens," Papa told Mama. Then he added meaningfully, "Three less to take along."

Desty's step jerked slightly at his words. But she knew they could not take an entire coopful of chickens. There were too many.

The day passed in a bustle of hurry and excitement. The thought of seeing dear Aunt Bessie again was a happy one and very comforting to Desty. Aunt Bessie would tell them about her trip. Maybe she would bring her a book. Aunt Bessie shared her love of reading. Perhaps they could plan to sew something together as they often did — but no, she could not plan anything too far in the future. She would be leaving Aunt Bessie when they moved to the Strip.

Suppertime came all too soon, but everything was ready. The whole family was waiting out front when Uncle Luke brought his carriage to a stop. When he helped Aunt Bessie down from the seat, her eyes were sparkling and happy. Then he bowed elegantly and said mischievously, "My wife, Mrs. Luke Andrews."

Everyone laughed at his teasing and Aunt Bessie's

cheeks grew pink. She said, "Oh, Luke," in a shy way and then hugged Mama tightly.

After everyone had kissed the new bride, Mama said, "Well, let's go inside, for goodness sake. Where are our manners, having our guests standing outside!"

Uncle Luke escorted Aunt Bessie through the door in a very proud way. Dressed in his store-bought clothes, he seemed more like a city man than a farmer. His stiff, stubborn hair was slicked down, and Desty thought he looked quite handsome. At the table he held Aunt Bessie's chair for her, then rubbed his palms together and said to Mama, "My, that smells good, Nell."

The dinner really did smell good. It looked good, too — stewed chicken and dumplings, hot biscuits and melted butter, currant jelly and two big cherry pies with lattice crusts on their tops.

All day Desty had been hungry for those tasty things as she and Fiddle helped Mama prepare them. There were cups and saucers at their places too, instead of glasses of milk. That meant Mama was going to let them have some coffee. This *was* a special occasion! The board had to be put in the big round table to have room for everyone. Best of all, she was going to sit beside Aunt Bessie.

Finally everyone was seated, and waited with bowed heads as Papa said grace. Then before anyone could start a conversation, Papa said loudly and happily, "Well, Luke, how do you like the idea of our family going home-steading?"

After that, the chicken and dumplings did not seem as delicious to Desty as she thought they would. But such a feast was too seldom a thing in the Shawn house to let anything spoil it for long.

Uncle Luke began to give his opinion on land rushes, and the Cherokee Strip, and before long, it was settled that he would lend Papa a horse named Duke. "With Champ and Duke hitched to the buckboard, you'll be the fastest thing next to the race horses," he declared.

Papa agreed, looking very happy. "Sure will, and Star is a good strong horse. He'll do fine with the wagon."

When the conversation stopped for a moment, Desty smiled at Aunt Bessie. "Are you and Uncle Luke going homesteading sometime, too?"

"Perhaps we will someday, Desty," Aunt Bessie answered. "But not right now."

"Let Aunt Bessie enjoy her dinner," Mama said. Then she added to Aunt Bessie: "Henry and I have some plans we want to talk over with you and Luke this evening. About where you will live." Mama's head nodded a little, her eyebrows arched and her look seemed to say something that her lips did not.

Aunt Bessie seemed puzzled, but she smiled. "Oh, that will be fine."

After supper Mama and Papa took their guests into the parlor with extra cups of coffee. The boys went outside to finish the chores, and Mama said Desty and Fiddle were to do the dishes immediately. That meant that the grown folks did not want to be disturbed. Desty was disappointed. She had hoped to find out the secret that was becoming bigger and bigger. She would explode with curiosity if she did not learn soon what it was!

All day it had just been between Mama and Papa — a promise that made Mama decide to go homesteading after working so hard here to put this house in such a nice condition.

Once, Desty had heard the boys say that each house

they moved to was less nice than the one before. Somehow that sounded as though the family had not succeeded very much. But all over the country there was something folks called the "Panic" — hard times. Work was scarce, therefore money was scarce too, and so were all the things that money could buy. So, why leave and go to less than they had?

She gave up trying to think of a reason for anything. Besides, Fiddle was shoving a wet cup at her.

"Hurry up, or we'll never get done," Fiddle complained. It was easy to see she was curious, too.

Desty dried the dishes faster from then on. Fiddle always wanted to wash because she said she could speed up the job. Desty did not blame her though. And this evening there was a real reason; they both were aching to join the grownups and find out what they were discussing.

Now, Desty thought, Aunt Bessie and Uncle Luke were also involved. But if they were not going to join them in the Cherokee Strip, then what *was* the secret?

"There, everything is washed," Fiddle announced triumphantly. "Hurry up and finish while I throw the water out." She took the dishpan to the back step and with a swish emptied it across the yard.

A howl rose out of the dusk. As Fiddle backed into the kitchen, Burt came running at her. Crumbs and greasy water dripped from every inch of his shirt. Trying to escape his reach, Fiddle bumped Desty and knocked a plate from her hand. The clatter and commotion brought Mama and Papa speedily from the parlor.

Mama guessed what happened right away. "Why didn't you take the dishwater all the way to the drain as you're supposed to, Fiddle?" The drain was just a little ditch at the far side of the dooryard where the thirsty earth quickly absorbed the water.

Papa was twisting his mouth this way and that, trying to keep from laughing. But he could not, and soon everyone joined in, except Burt. Even Aunt Bessie and Uncle Luke had rushed to the kitchen and were now doubling over in laughter. Desty did not want to laugh, because she saw how miserable and foolish Burt felt, but she could not help it.

Mama raised her hand for quiet. "Burt, take that shirt off and put it in the washbasket behind the door. I'll wash it in the morning."

Then Mama led the way back to the parlor. After everyone was settled on the dark green plush sofa, the chairs, or ottoman, she looked knowingly at Aunt Bessie. Then she said, "You girls must be more careful with the dishes because we want to leave enough for Aunt Bessie and Uncle Luke to use."

What a strange thing for Mama to say. Before Mama could explain, Fiddle asked, "What do you mean, Mama?" Then before Mama could answer, Fiddle looked quickly to Papa.

Papa grinned widely, smoothing back his bushy hair. "Mama means that Aunt Bessie and Uncle Luke are going to live here and use our things when we leave for the Cherokee Strip."

"Then if the claim doesn't work out well," Mama added, looking straight at Papa, "we'll have a home to come back to. And that way we don't have to take everything with us." She smiled at Aunt Bessie. "If we settle permanently down there, Aunt Bessie will send us what we want of the things we will leave behind. That way Uncle Luke and Aunt Bessie will have a place to live by themselves until they plan their own home later on."

Now Desty knew what Papa had promised Mama — no more moving on to new places after this next one in the Strip. The Strip would have to prove best for them or they would move back to this house. She felt much better in a way. Yet if things went well in the Strip, they would stay there — but she would not think of that now.

When Uncle Luke and Aunt Bessie were getting into the carriage to leave, Uncle Luke said, "Well, look here, would you! We plumb forgot to bring in the package." He handed a box down to Papa. "A few little things we picked up on our trip for you." Then with a flick of the whip, he and Aunt Bessie waved goodnight and drove off.

In the box were books for Fiddle and her, and for Burt and Jason. Hers was called *Little Women*. How wonderful! Really four new books to read, because she would borrow the others as soon as she finished her own.

Papa's gift was a pair of house slippers. He chuckled. "Luke and Bessie don't know me very well. I like to put my shoes on first thing in the morning, and take them off last thing at night. Always be ready, I say. Can't be ready if you get a 'too-settled-down' feeling —" He stopped suddenly when he looked at Mama.

Desty realized then that she had never seen Papa wear house slippers.

Mama's gift was a wind chime. It was made of many narrow strips of glass on which were painted flowers and leaves. They were tied with red string to a wooden frame.

"How lovely," Mama said, and she went to the door

and held it up in the warm evening breeze. The little glass panels swayed gently and touched each other, making the most beautiful tinkling sound.

Mama put it back in its box. "We'll keep it for our new home," she said.

## Chapter Four

# Goodbye, Marietta

Every day Papa made some new preparations for the trip. He overhauled the wagon completely so that it would hold up well. He strengthened and greased the buckboard. Mama sorted and packed every day too, clothes, linens, dishes, sewing articles and so on.

The land rush was to start at high noon on September sixteenth. The date was coming closer and closer. August ran out, and with each day that passed Desty felt as if something very precious were being snatched away from her.

Every time they had moved in the past, they had moved into a house that had already been built, surrounded by a certain amount of land which went with it.

Now where they were going there would be no house at all, just miles and miles of land. She almost hated to think of so much empty space.

As Papa often mentioned, they had come to Kansas four years before to be in the 1889 Run into the Oklahoma territory. When he fell sick, they rented this farm. It's such a nice place, too, she thought, with Mama's garden and flower beds. And when times got too hard for them on the farm, Papa always could go into Wellington or up to Wichita to work for a spell and earn some money.

Oh well, she thought, soon Papa would have his chance to be in a Run. But Papa's promise about moving back kept bothering her. That would be only if they had bad luck in the Strip. If things went well down there they would stay. If she wanted her dream of coming back to come true, then Papa's dream of homesteading would have to be shattered. When she thought of this, she felt as bad as she did before she knew of the promise.

The road that passed their house ran south a few miles and then veered west to meet the old Chisholm Trail. The town of Caldwell was on the trail, just north of the border of the Cherokee Strip.

She and Fiddle loved to hear the stories folks told about the Chisholm Trail. It was the road over which herds of cattle were driven from Texas to Abilene, Kansas. And since it came straight through the Oklahoma territory it also ran straight through the Cherokee Strip. But no cattle were herded over it that way any more. Railroads were mostly used to ship cattle now.

Ever since Papa had decided to be in the land rush, he stuck to the opinion that anyone making the Run down that old trail would make far better time than over the unbroken sod. So he planned to go to Caldwell and start from there.

Now they would see the Trail, and travel on it. But the idea did not appeal very much to Desty. Fiddle, however, gloated over it by the hour. "Just like the trail herders, down the old Chisholm Trail," she would chant.

Every day more and more travelers passed their house. "All making for the same spot, seems like," Papa said. "Some will be camping down there for weeks at the starting point. The sooner we leave, the better."

One day she and Fiddle were out in the barn watching Papa oil some harness. "How far is Caldwell, Papa?" Fiddle asked.

"Oh, about thirty to thirty-five miles as the crow flies."

"Will everybody who wants free land start out from Caldwell?"

"No," Papa answered. "Only a small part of the crowd. They'll be coming from starting points on all sides of the Strip — north, south, east and west. It sure will be a big race."

Desty still hoped that somehow they might make a return to Kansas. "What do the people do who don't get a claim?" she asked.

Papa hung the harness on a nail on the wall. "Some go into the town site and rent a spot from someone else, or buy out a homesteader who is leaving. Or they go back to where they came from."

The last part of Papa's explanation helped Desty to hope a little more.

Suddenly, it seemed, September thirteenth arrived. Everyone got up earlier than usual. All preparations would have to be completed so that by nightfall they would be as ready as they ever could be. Tomorrow at sunrise they would start.

Her few dresses, petticoats, underthings and stockings were packed in the trunk along with Mama's and Fiddle's. Their extra pair of shoes were put into a big canvas bag with Papa's and the boy's things.

They helped Mama pack enough of the dishes to use, a knife, fork, and spoon for each, a large and small fry pan, one big sauce pan and a large cooking kettle, coffee pot, and bread and pie pans.

Papa had fashioned a table top and legs which he could attach at their new place. He did the same with six stools. That way he could pack them into the wagon more easily. They stuffed folded blankets and their pillows in between to hold them tighter. Papa bought a small, round, second-hand iron stove. Everything had to take up as little room as possible in the wagon.

Mama's rocking chair was an exception. Papa saw Mama looking fondly at it and patted her shoulder. "That will go with us." When Mama protested that it might take up too much space, he held up his hand and inclined his head. "It is one comfort you shall have. It goes with us."

After lunch, Mama said it was time everyone rested a while.

Desty knew she could not rest. "I'm not tired, Mama. May Fiddle and I go now to say goodbye to Marietta?"

"Of course, but don't walk too fast in the hot sun. And don't stay too long. Tell Mrs. Hobson Papa and I will be over this evening to say goodbye."

On the way Desty tried to picture being outdoors like

this with no house anywhere to go into. Of course, in the Strip everyone would build a shelter of some kind, but until they did it would be just open country.

By the time they reached Marietta's gate, she was already missing everything they would have to leave behind. Most of all, she did not want to say goodbye to Marietta. "I wish we hadn't come," she said.

Fiddle was reaching over to pet little Bouncey's head. She jerked up impatiently. "Why? For goodness sake, we walked all the way over here. Besides, it's the last time we'll see Marietta."

"I know." She followed Fiddle and Bouncey up the newly-painted steps. Marietta's folks were always painting and fixing their home, so that it looked like something out of a storybook. The grass was always cut to the right height too, as if it never grew any higher. The cushions on the porch swing were always in the right position, fluffed up invitingly.

She looked around and knew that she would miss these pleasant surroundings almost as much as she would miss Marietta herself.

"Well, hello!" a gay voice called. It was Mrs. Hobson's. She opened the screen door. "My, but it's warm this afternoon. Marietta will be here in a minute." She motioned to the swing and a little table nearby. "Sit down and have some lemonade and cookies."

The cold drink felt wonderful to Desty's dry throat. She and Fiddle helped themselves to the delicious cookies on the tray. Soon Marietta, looking very cool and comfortable in a pink cotton dress, came out on the porch. She held two thin packages.

"I'm so glad you came. But if you didn't I would have

gone to your place." She handed them each a package. "They are just little going-away presents." Marietta choked on the last words and Desty knew how she felt.

"Thank you, Marietta," Fiddle said brightly, but Desty just looked her gratitude. She knew her voice would sound shaky. Fiddle undid the wrapping immediately and found a lovely white handkerchief edged with pointed lace. Desty's was the same except that her lace was scalloped. She held it against her throat, "I will keep it forever," she promised.

They did not stay long, as Mama had asked them not to. Before they left the porch, Marietta hugged them both and ran back into the house. She was crying.

Desty could not push the picture of Marietta's sad face out of her mind. All the way home she could see it, and pitied Marietta because now she would be without playmates. Desty herself would always have Fiddle.

After they reached their house, Fiddle spent most of the late afternoon out at the barn watching Papa and the boys doing the chores and making last minute checks on their preparations.

Desty stayed in the house. She was alone with Mama. "Do you really want to move, Mama?" she asked.

"No, not really. It is hard to start over at anything."

"Well, why don't we stay here where we have a house and everything?" There must be a reason, and she had to know. Maybe knowing would make her feel better.

"Because it is Papa's dream to own his own place someday," Mama answered. "A man's dream is his goal, and we have to help Papa reach his."

She admired Mama's loyalty, but she still could not see the sense in what seemed like going from bad to worse.

Mama continued: "Papa wants the best for all of us, and it is never easy to get the best." Somehow those words *did* make sense to Desty.

"Well, then why don't we all just stay here until Papa stakes a claim and comes back for us?" she asked.

"Because we can help Papa more if we're near him, especially if anything goes wrong."

Desty thought of Uncle Gus and his losing out in the other run. "What if Papa doesn't get a claim?"

"Oh," Mama assured her, "with Champ and Duke, Papa is almost sure of getting a fine quarter-section."

While Mama was talking, she poured a cup of coffee for herself. Then she poured a second cup. They were the only ones in the house. Perhaps Mama would say to call Papa in to rest a while. But no, Mama smiled and said, "It is time we ladies took a little bit of refreshment."

How wonderful Mama was, she thought, treating her like a grownup. And she felt every inch a lady, joining Mama in having a cup of coffee. Perhaps, she told herself, if she tried hard enough, she could see homesteading in a grown-up way, and then it would not seem nearly so bad.

## Chapter Five

# "It's Kansas Earth"

The fourteenth of September dawned bright and rosy. This was the morning they would leave home. When Papa's jovial voice boomed up the stairway, "Come on, everybody, time to get up!" Desty awoke immediately.

She could not snuggle down for a few more minutes to let herself wake up slowly and easily. And she could not pout about being called extra early. She had slept her last night in this house. She looked hungrily around the little bedroom, trying to remember every detail. She wanted to remember forever the way it looked.

She thought of Papa's promise to return. But she could scarcely be consoled by that. Things had to turn out wrong for Papa to keep that promise. If they had good fortune, they would never come back to Kansas.

When she was certain she could face the day and the immense change that it would bring to her family, she got up and dressed. She knew Fiddle had not fully awakened yet, because if Fiddle had realized what day it was, she would have bounded out of bed.

Desty touched her shoulder, then shook her gently.

"It's time to get up."

"This early?"

"Yes, we have — to start early." She felt her throat tightening at the words.

Fiddle was still half asleep. "Start early?" And then her eyes widened. "Oh yes!" And she *did* bound out of bed with one leap.

Fiddle dressed so hurriedly she put her dress on backwards. She jerked it off over her head and started again. But when she tried to fasten it, she found the buttons were on the inside. Now she had it on inside-out!

"Oh, jumping grasshoppers!" And again, angrily and hastily she pulled the dress off. On the third attempt she got it on correctly and buttoned up right. Then she grabbed her stockings and drew them on so fast they twisted. Her toes went promptly into the heel.

"Why can't we just go barefoot?" she complained.

Desty handed her the other stocking. "Because Mama wants us to look properly dressed on the trip."

After much struggling, Fiddle succeeded in straightening her stockings well enough to suit herself. Then she almost jumped into her shoes, closing them with the top, bottom and middle buttons only, leaving the rest to gape apart.

Desty waited, watching Fiddle's performance. Fiddle had taken more time to dress this morning than ever before, even though she hurried more.

Downstairs, all was hustle and bustle. Mama would not think of leaving until they all had a substantial breakfast in their stomachs. She made oatmeal and toast, and milk and coffee as usual. There also was fruit, plus bacon and eggs. Yet the morning was filled with high excitement and the boys, especially, wanted to skimp on the time taken for breakfast.

But Mama insisted. "Everyone must eat plenty. Noontime is a long way off."

Papa glanced at Desty's plate, which she scarcely touched. "Here, here, Desty, you must eat more than that."

She reached for her toast and tried to eat some of it, but she really did not feel like eating anything at all.

Papa patted her shoulder as though he understood. Then he coaxed, "You must have something that sticks to your ribs."

"Ha, ha," Jason laughed. "I don't want something that only sticks to my ribs. I want something that sticks to all of me."

That struck Fiddle funny and she laughed before she could swallow her milk. She groped for her napkin and drenched it when she opened her mouth because she began to choke.

Mama slapped her on the back. "No more jokes, please."

Fiddle's face grew red but she still laughed squeakily. Desty had to grin, too, and Papa smiled as he pushed the oatmeal away, and put a plate of bacon and eggs in front of her. After one taste, her appetite sharpened and she ate all of it.

Papa and the boys wolfed their food down so quickly

that Mama just shook her head as she watched them. Then they left the table and hurried outdoors. Mama lingered a while with the girls, but in a moment or two, Fiddle ran out to join the boys. Left alone with Mama, Desty felt her mother's nearness very comforting. Neither one said anything, but Mama reached over and pressed Desty's arm. Then she straightened Desty's pinafore ruffles.

Desty and Fiddle were wearing their dark blue cotton dresses topped by dark blue pinafores which would not show the dust too easily. They were going to carry their warm sweaters which Mama and Aunt Bessie had knit for them last Christmas. They would need them in the coolness of the evening, Mama said. How far away would they be this evening, Desty wondered.

Mama pressed her arm again. "You mustn't worry or feel bad about anything, Desty. Whatever we can't change, we can learn to live with. Something helps us to, so whatever happens, don't fret." Desty's throat felt too tight to answer, and she was glad that at that moment Fiddle burst through the doorway. Fiddle was restless. She fidgeted with her pinafore ties. She sat down and then got up again. Mama asked her if she did not find anything to do out at the wagon.

Fiddle shrugged her shoulders. "They won't let me. Boys think they know everything, so let them do everything."

Mama laughed shortly and said she had to attend to some "last minute things" upstairs like checking to see that she had taken down all the items they needed for the journey. Also to see if she had left everything in places where Aunt Bessie could find them.

Surveying the table, Fiddle picked up a slice of cold toast and nibbled at it. Then she drank some more milk. "Now, I'm finished for sure," she announced, flicking her napkin across her lips.

Before Fiddle could get up from her chair, Desty reminded her, "We have to do the dishes."

Then behind them, she heard someone say, "You don't have to do the dishes. I'll do them later." It was Aunt Bessie. She and Uncle Luke stood in the doorway. "And don't look so surprised, girls," she added laughing. "You didn't think I'd let you leave without saying goodbye."

"Oh, Aunt Bessie, I'm so glad you came." Desty ran to hug her pink-cheeked young aunt, whom she loved more than anyone next to Mama and Papa. Even a little more than Fiddle sometimes, she admitted to herself, feeling guilty.

"So am I," Fiddle joined in, hugging her aunt from the other side.

Aunt Bessie laughed delightedly and then put her hands on Fiddle's shoulders and gently moved her back to her chair. Stooping down, she buttoned Fiddle's shoes properly. After she looked over the rest of Fiddle's clothing she gave her a little shooing pat towards the door.

Fiddle giggled. "You didn't have to bother, Aunt Bessie. Mama would have made me fix my shoes before we left." She ran outside.

Aunt Bessie turned to Desty and smiled. "I brought you and Fiddle and the boys some extra slate pencils. You won't have to do without drawing and writing when your old ones wear out."

That was so like Aunt Bessie, to try to take a little cheer wherever she went. She talked about many things, but not about anything that could remind a person of moving or homesteading. She told Desty of the new kittens at Uncle Luke's place, and about the beautiful hats she saw in Wichita on her honeymoon. And about the lovely ride through the wooded countryside in a carriage Uncle Luke rented for a day.

All the while, though, Desty was conscious of Papa and the boys hurrying through the kitchen carrying different items. They kept saying, "Don't forget the broom," or "Don't forget the milk jug," or "Take a couple of old potato sacks too, they'll come in handy." They bumped into each other occasionally. Papa checked out the food supplies packed in the wagon. Burt marked the list he had written: two sacks of coffee beans, a jug of molasses, sugar, flour, salted sidemeat, two smoked hams, a big tin of lard, salt, and canteens of water besides the big water barrel.

Uncle Luke joined in and carried Mama's rocking chair out. It was to go into the wagon last so that it could be reached easily when they stopped for the evening.

Outside, Jason could be heard telling Fiddle to scat, to get out of the way, to go back into the house. But Aunt Bessie went on telling of pleasant things. Finally Mama came downstairs again. She hugged Aunt Bessie and looked at them both as if ready to say something. But she only smiled and started a final inspection of downstairs. When she finished she picked up a basket containing fried chicken and several loaves of bread to eat on the way. Then she held out her hand to Desty.

"I guess we got just about everything. We better go now."

Desty put her palms flat on the chair and raised herself slowly, took Mama's hand on one side and Aunt Bessie's on the other. But they quickly let go of each other at the doorway as Fiddle raced through, nearly knocking them over.

Fiddle grabbed Desty's arm. "Our treasure boxes, we forgot them!"

Before she could excuse herself to Mama or Aunt Bessie, Fiddle pulled her towards the stairs. They had deliberately left the boxes until last so that they would not get hidden under anything in the packing. Up in their room, Desty gently held her beloved cigar box with the curlicues painted on its cover. She knew by heart what was in it — a pretty card, a short piece of bright red ribbon, two marbles, a pencil stub and two smooth sparkly stones.

She looked at all the treasures and then firmly closed the lid. Fiddle was already running down the stairs, stopping only long enough to shout back, "Hurry up!"

When Desty reached the kitchen again, it was empty. Everyone had gone outside. She took a long last look at the stove, remembering all the oatmeal and vegetables it had cooked, and all the bread and cakes it had baked. She felt as if she were leaving a dear, warm friend. Then her look rested on the table, the chairs, the woodbox.

Suddenly Fiddle was calling again, "Hurry up, Desty."

It was best to leave quickly, she thought, so out the doorway she stepped, down the porch steps and on toward the wagon. Fiddle was already up on the seat between Mama and Jason, shifting this way and that in her eagerness to get going.

Everyone seemed to be ready to move out. Aunt Bessie

came over and hugged her but she did not say goodbye. "Now, we'll write each other letters and tell each other about everything. Promise?" Aunt Bessie's sparkling eyes seemed to say don't worry, everything will turn out just wonderfully.

Desty nodded her head in promise.

Then Uncle Luke stepped up, took Desty's hand in his two rough, calloused palms, patted it and said, "Be a good girl and nothing can go wrong." His stiff, stubborn brown hair stuck out over his forehead a little even with his hat on. He had visited their family often ever since they moved to Kansas, but she could not remember having liked him so much as at that moment.

Papa was waiting to help her up to the wagon seat. As he took her arm, she suddenly recalled the story Mama told of a little Irish girl leaving her home for America. The girl took along a piece of sod from her father's farm so that she would always have a little bit of Ireland near her.

Brushing Papa's hand aside for a moment, Desty flipped up the lid of her treasure box, bent over and scooped up a handful of earth. She tossed it into the box and closed it. Then she turned to Papa and let him help her onto the wagon.

Fiddle had been watching her. "Are you crazy, Desty? Throwing dirt all over your treasures?"

"It's Kansas earth," Desty answered without looking at her. She hoped no one else would mention it. No one did. Out of the corner of her eye she could see Fiddle shrug her shoulders. But she did not expect Fiddle to understand. This was one of the times Fiddle seemed like a little sister, instead of her twin.

There was a fluttering sound in the wagon, then the loud cluck-cluck of the hens in a crate set on top of the piled-up household articles. Bossy, their milk cow, was tied to the back of the wagon.

There were things packed on the buckboard too, on which Papa and Burt would ride. Jason was to drive the wagon with Mama and the girls.

Now all was ready. Papa went to the buckboard and climbed up beside Burt. He lifted the reins and snapped them down, calling, "Giddap" to Champ and Duke. Jason did the same on the wagon and they began to move slowly down the road which would take them to Caldwell.

Everyone was calling goodbye to Aunt Bessie and Uncle Luke, and they were answering with "Good luck" and "Godspeed." Desty only waved, then she stared straight ahead as they drove away.

## Chapter Six

# Granny Buckskin

The day was bright with sunshine, and the clean smell of morning was all around them. If she could think only of those things, Desty told herself, she might feel very differently about moving. But after the first hour the ride grew tiresome. They had started later than Papa had planned, and now the sun was climbing high.

Mama said it was too crowded with four on the seat. "I'll sit inside for a spell," she told Jason. He stopped the horses until Mama climbed back under the canvas top.

Fiddle's excitement was as high as ever. She kept up a report of everything they passed. Once she saw a jack rabbit, then a prairie dog. Then she heard a lark, followed by a mockingbird call. When Jason clucked his tongue to Star, Fiddle called "Giddap!" And all the while the warm wind swept by them, making the tall grass sway as though it were keeping time to a tune.

But the morning seemed terribly long and the day seemed much hotter sitting high up on a wagon seat. When she felt she could stand it no longer, Mama told her and Fiddle to come inside out of the sun, and changed places with them on the seat.

Jason stopped the horses again long enough to roll up the canvas along the sides and tie it to the bows so that the wind could course through.

"I should have done that before for *you*, Mama," he said.

"Oh, no, I enjoyed the shade, and I sat in the middle so that I got the breeze going through from front to back."

Papa and Burt looked back over their shoulders just as Jason was starting up again, and he gave them a wave that everything was all right.

Desty lay down on the bedding and soon the rolling motion soothed her to sleep. She dreamed she was going on a long trip to a castle in Europe, and that the ocean voyage was so rough she was overwhelmed with joy when she reached the other side.

Then, suddenly, she was jarred out of her sleep by loud shouts and a banging noise. "Come and get it! Come and get it!" She sat up immediately. What in the world was that! The wagon had stopped.

She looked out over the wagon side and there was Fiddle, yelling at the top of her voice, and striking a pan with a wooden spoon. Mama was waving her hand in protest. "Hush, Fiddle, you'll wake the dead with that racket."

Now Desty could smell the coffee that was cooking over an open fire. It was lunchtime. The horses were grazing, though still in harness, and Papa and the boys were coming towards the wagon.

"Well, there it is — the Chisholm Trail." Papa pointed to the west of them. Desty could see only a road not much different than the one over which they rode all morning. The grass grew up in the middle between the wheel tracks in the same way.

Fiddle began to chant, "The Chisholm Trail, the Chisholm Trail, the Chisholm, Chisholm, Chisolm Trail!"

Papa laughed and told her to settle down. There was prairie land on either side, with its high, lush grass bending to and fro endlessly. Then the sweeping wind brought the lonesome wail of a train whistle.

Soon Mama called them together and passed out pieces of corn bread and fried chicken from the basket. But before anyone could start eating, she made them all bow their heads, just as at home.

As Desty ate, she remembered her dream. Thank goodness she was not going that far away from home. Home? There was no "home" any more, really. Again, the ache settled in her like an itch that she could not scratch away. From farther away now, she could still hear the train whistle sing out across the prairie.

Before they started off again, two other parties came along and went on after a brief stop. The first was a family with five children. In the second party, there were two men on horseback, who had left their families behind until they could settle and send for them. They talked and exchanged information with Papa about the land rush.

On their way during the afternoon they met many more, all headed in the same direction. Some knew a great deal more than others about the homesteading business, and some were as "green" as Papa said he himself was.

Most of them, however, wasted no more time on visiting than they had to to be polite. There was a hurried air about them. Desty could feel their anxiety. They were all trying to beat each other to the border line.

About two miles north of Caldwell, they met many who had set up camp for the night. Papa said it would be a good idea for them to spend the night there too, after an early supper. They pulled off to the east side of the road and started a fire.

The boys unhitched the horses and untied the cow and hobbled them. Papa strode off to scout a little. He said he wanted to find where the crowds were thickest so that he could figure out just what part of the line to head for.

It was good to get down on the ground again, Desty felt. She began to help Mama prepare supper, but Fiddle wanted to run off to explore all around their campsite.

"You will stay here and help Desty and me make supper," Mama said firmly.

"Aw, gee," Fiddle complained, but she took the plates and cups out of the hamper and placed them on the tailgate of the wagon until Mama was ready to fill them. When Papa came back, they laid a blanket on the grass and sat down.

As they ate, more and more landseekers stopped to make camp close by.

One tall, lanky fellow dismounted near them and spoke to Papa. "Seems like everybody thinks the same. They all want to start from Caldwell." He held out his hand to Papa. "Name's Smith."

"I'm Hank Shawn — my family," Papa answered, gesturing towards Mama and the rest of them. "You're right about Caldwell. And it seems to be more crowded on the west side of the town. I guess we'll have to back off a little to the east to get a good place on the line."

"Guess so," Smith said. He stood beside his horse and munched on a sandwich which he took from his saddle bag. Then he mounted and left. They never saw him again.

Desty looked out over all the campers and wondered which ones, if any, they would see at the line, in the Strip, or ever again anywhere.

After supper she and Fiddle got a chance to roam around a little.

"Not too far," Mama warned them. Folks were visiting with each other all over the place, and when she looked back, a man and a woman were stopping by for a chat with Mama and Papa.

Some of the children they saw were friendly. But some of the others were just the opposite. There was one freckled-face, straggly-haired boy who sneered every time he looked at her and Fiddle. Finally, twisting his lips in an ugly way, he yelled, "Carrot-tops, Carrot-Tops, Carrot-T —."

She turned away from him. But then she looked back quickly to see why he stopped so suddenly. And there was Fiddle, her fists doubled up, rushing at him. He stumbled and fell and while he was down on his hands and knees, Fiddle pummeled his back as hard as she could.

He was getting just what he deserved. Desty thought.

But what if he turned and fought back? She must help Fiddle. She was starting forward, when Mama, looking very ashamed, ran ahead of her and pulled Fiddle upright.

"What in the world has gotten into you," Mama said.

The boy, gaining his feet, backed off looking defiantly at them. "Carrot-tops, that's all you are."

Then behind them Desty heard a voice calling, "Emerson, Emerson, come on back here." The boy ran towards a thin woman in a limp sunbonnet and faded apron. She walked with shuffling steps as though her knees were wired together and only the lower part of her legs moved. She put her arm around the boy's shoulders and leaned forward to speak to him. Then she gave Desty and Fiddle a look that seemed to say they were nothing but trouble-makers.

Fiddle laughed. "Emerson, what a name!" Then she raised her voice and yelled, "Goodbye, Emmy!"

The boy jerked in his tracks.

Mama grasped Fiddle's arm. "That is enough!" Her face was angry as she marched Fiddle back to the wagon.

Jason and Burt were seeing to the horses and Papa was just about to stamp out the fire when another wagon pulled up so close it almost touched theirs.

On its seat sat a plump little woman in a buckskin jacket and riding skirt. Looking up at her, Desty could see her feet resting on the footboard. She was wearing Indian moccasins. On her head was a well-worn man's felt hat.

"Hello, there," the woman said in a rich, bell-like tone. Next to Mama's and Aunt Bessie's soft voices, this woman had quite the most likeable voice Desty had ever heard.

The woman strode over to Papa with much longer steps than her short legs seemed able to take. "Do you mind leaving the fire burn? I'm dying for a cup of coffee." She went to the back of her wagon and reached inside.

"No, no," Mama said, when she saw a coffee pot in the woman's hand. "Don't make any. You can share ours."

"That's very kind of you. Thank you." Her words were clear and even. She sounded much different than she looked, Desty thought.

The woman's face, tanned and lined by wind and sun, spread into a wide smile. Her lively, dark eyes almost disappeared into the plump folds above her cheeks. Now her face reminded Desty of the ones she and Fiddle used to make with Mama's fruit bread before baking, when they pushed raisins into the dough for eyes, nose and mouth.

The woman pulled off the felt hat and brushed back her graying black hair. Her thick brows were getting gray too. Jason brought her a stool.

Mama poured a cup of coffee. "We're the Shawn family. My husband, Henry, our boys, Burt and Jason, and our twins, Desty and Fiddle."

Being introduced to a stranger was always a nice experience, but Desty could not help feeling shy, so she only nodded. Fiddle smiled, Burt jerked his head slightly and Jason waved and said "Howdy" as Papa did.

The woman smiled again. "I'm Molly Savannah. But just call me Granny Buckskin as everyone else does — on account of this." She touched the jacket lightly. "It belonged to my husband, Jeremiah Savannah." The proud way she spoke the name made her seem taller, almost royal, Desty thought. How odd, because Granny, with her flat Indian moccasins on her feet, was a head shorter than Mama.

After Granny finished her coffee, she brought a knapsack from her wagon, and handed some crisp, brown spice cookies to Desty, Fiddle and the boys. And another wide smile made her eyes look tiny.

But when Granny's face was sober again, her eyes seemed much larger as she looked out across the prairie. She appeared to be searching the horizon.

Desty had a feeling that Granny's eyes had seen a great deal in her lifetime. How wonderful would be the stories she could tell! But she was just a passing traveler. Maybe they would never see her after this evening.

While Granny and Mama were talking, Papa walked around Granny's wagon, looking over the water barrel, buckets, tub, wooden stool, two chairs all strapped to the outside of the wagon. The inside looked as though it were pretty full too. Here and there the canvas bulged out over the wagon edge.

Papa shook his ahead. "That's a heavy load to make the Run with. You won't get far."

Granny explained. "Just going to Caldwell. I'll leave my belongings there and take the train for the Run. I want a town site if I can get one. When my claim is safe, I'll come back for my things."

"Is the train going to be in the land rush too?" Fiddle asked. She always seemed to forget that Mama taught them to sit quietly by while grown-ups visited.

Granny did not seem to mind. "It sure is. It runs right through some of the sites mapped out for towns." She turned to Mama. "I want to set up a laundry business if I can — the Jeremiah Savannah Laundry." Again she

spoke the name proudly, squaring her shoulders notice-
ably, as though there were magic in the mentioning of
her husband's name.

Granny went on to explain, and then Desty knew that
her own feeling about Granny's ability to tell stories was
correct.

"We made the Run in 1889," Granny said. "We got
a claim and were jumped by a gang of thieves. They
wounded Jeremiah. There was no doctor near, but I don't
think it would have mattered anyhow. The wound was
too serious. After Jeremiah died, I went back to Wichita
to live with our daughter's family." Suddenly Granny
looked very tired. Then just as suddenly, she squared her
shoulders again. "Jeremiah was half white and half
Cherokee. He always wanted to own some land. He was
the best man I ever knew."

Again she looked out over the area dotted with campers of every description, but she looked as if she were
seeing much, much more.

When she did not say anything further, Mama and
Papa wished her good luck in this Run. They also told
her they would look her up afterwards if at all possible.

Suddenly Papa said, "I have a livery stable in mind
myself. Maybe I could rent space from you in town, after
I get our homestead going."

Desty loved Papa very much right then. His idea
would connect their family with Granny. It would be
almost like having relatives in the Strip.

"Be glad to." Granny snapped out her answer as
though she were waiting for such an offer.

The sun had set and twilight was stealing over the
land. Granny rose and went toward her wagon. "I'd like

to get into Caldwell for the night. It won't be too hard to get through now. There aren't very many on the road."

Her moccasins made soft padding sounds. Papa helped her up to the wagon seat. She waved, calling, "Good luck. We'll see each other again."

What a wonderful way to end the day, Desty thought.

## Chapter Seven

# Emmy Again

The next day they were all up bright and early. In a few hours they would arrive at the line.

While they prepared to leave, Papa tried to remember everything Uncle Gus had said about the land in the Strip.

"There were some good spots on both sides of the Chisholm Trail. If we start from the east side and angle southwest, we will have a chance to see some of both sides. If we don't get a chance on the eastern side, we can take the trail south for a ways and then strike west." Papa scratched his head as though he could not remember well enough. "Seems to me Gus mentioned a place with water and trees."

Desty hoped their claim would have water and trees, not just empty land.

When they reached the line, the crowd was so thick they had to go farther east about a mile and a half.

Papa did not worry about that though. "Once the signal is given, and we pull ahead of the heavy wagons and slower saddle horses, we'll have plenty of room."

Jason spit in the dust. It was a habit Mama scolded him for, but she did not see him this time. "Champ and Duke will beat all of them except the real race horses," he said smiling.

Even Burt seemed to catch the excitement. He patted both horses' manes. "Sure will," he said.

Papa unhitched the horses but left the buckboard right on the line to keep his place. The wagon was a little ways behind it. While they made camp, folks kept drifting in from all directions. The saddle horses and riders were countless; but there were also many light vehicles, such as buckboards like Papa's, carriages, two-wheeled carts, surreys and sulkies. There were covered wagons like theirs, and heavier ones, and lighter spring wagons, too.

The more crowded the area became, the denser the dust grew, until it seemed to rise like a cloud ready to choke them. But there was an awful smoky smell, too, in the air.

"Folks say it's because the ones in charge burned the thick, tangled grass off the land so that the prairie dog holes and uneven spots could be seen easier," Papa explained.

"Yes, and to chase sooners out, too," Burt added. He was smiling again.

"What's a sooner, Papa?" Fiddle wanted to know.

"That's someone who hides in the Strip ahead of time so he doesn't have to make the Run. Then he stakes a claim before the others get there." Papa's face looked a little angry as he spoke.

Just then, two weather-browned, straggly-haired old-timers drove by in a rickety wagon. "That old Chisholm Trail ain't been churned up like that in a long time," one said to the other. They both raised their leathery hands in salute to Papa as they passed, and smiled to Desty and Fiddle. Desty could see that both had only a few tobacco-stained teeth and their hair was gray, but no one she had seen on the journey had seemed happier than they.

Fiddle asked Papa, "Is this where the Run starts?"

"This is the spot where we'll start from. All these folks will line up on either side of us."

Then Fiddle asked, "What are those soldiers riding around for?" She pointed to the blue-coated calvary men patroling in front of the line.

Papa patted her head. "To see that no one starts before time."

According to Mama's instructions, Jason and Burt were hanging canvas from the wagon bed to the ground. They would sleep under the wagon tonight, and the canvas would keep some of the dust out. Mama and the girls would sleep in the wagon as they did last night, and Papa would stay with the buckboard.

The people with no wagons mostly had tents. But some of the men had only bedrolls. When Desty looked around at all the hustle and bustle she wished more than ever that they were back on their farm. But Mama had said you must live with what you can't change, so she made up her mind to make the best of it — if she could.

After they rested and had some lunch, Papa saddled up Champ. "Well, I guess it's high time I went to register."

Everyone who was seeking a claim had to go to the rough board booths or tents dotted along the border, to get a registration certificate. It would do a person no good to make the Run and stake a claim if he did not have a certificate. It would be needed to file the claim afterwards at the land office. Papa said that was how you received title to the one hundred sixty acres of a quarter section.

Papa motioned to Burt to go along with him. Burt mounted Duke. But when Papa saw the wishful look on Jason's face, he laughed and said, "All right, you may as well come along. Nothing can happen to Mama and the girls while we're gone."

Jason climbed up on Star's back. Both boys rode bareback.

While they were gone, Desty and Fiddle helped Mama take out the bedrolls and put them under the wagon for the boys. Then Mama built up the fire and cooked a big kettle of cornmeal mush to have with sorghum molasses for supper. Whatever was left over would be put away to fry for breakfast.

But Papa and the boys did not come back for supper.

Mama kept glancing westward, in the direction of the registration booth. It was just south of Caldwell across the border. "They must be waiting in an awfully long line to be so late," she said.

Then she told Desty and Fiddle to sit up on the wagon

seat where they could see better and to let her know when
they saw Papa and the boys coming. "I might be able to
heat their supper a little by the time they get here."

The sun was sinking down out of sight like a giant red
ball on its littlest, last bounce. Desty thought of what
used to be home and fought off a wave of homesickness.
Since she could not wish Papa to have bad luck in something he wanted so much, there was only one thing to do
— she had to try to like the Strip.

Then she thought of Marietta and wondered what she
was doing now. Probably sitting out on her front porch
with her mother and father having lemonade and cookies.
Or maybe playing with Bouncey. She had to stop thinking of such things.

Twilight inched slowly over the crowds clustered
around hundreds of campfires. The noise and din continued. Back home, everything would be sort of hushed
now, and here and there a late bird would be flying by,
giving a last few chirps as though calling its family together. Mama would be saying that the birds were going
home to rest. And that would mean that she and Fiddle
should be getting ready for bed too. But here it was different. They seemed just part of a big, noisy crowd.

She almost fell off the wagon seat when Fiddle jumped
up, shouting to Mama, "Here they come! I see them, here
they come!"

Desty strained her eyes in the gloom and then she saw
Papa and the boys weaving through the throngs of
shadowy figures.

After they climbed down from the wagon seat, Fiddle
asked Mama if they could join some boys and girls who

were running and playing a few campsites away. Mama shook her head. "They sound too rough. It would be best to keep away from them."

Again Desty thought of Marietta and what a nice playmate she was. But she wished they could do something. "Let's see if there are any fireflies," she said.

Fiddle laughed. "They would all be scared away by now. If I weren't any bigger than a firefly I would make a hole in the ground and crawl into it until all these folks got out of here."

That was what Desty wished she could do herself, but she could not tell Fiddle that. Fiddle would not understand. She knew Mama would, but she did not want to talk to Mama about it and make her feel sad.

They walked a little way among the campsites and suddenly Fiddle stopped. "Look, there's that ugly boy, Emmy."

He was running in their direction. Desty caught Fiddle's arm to pull her back towards the wagon. "Don't you dare say a word to him."

She certainly did not want to see Fiddle in a common fist fight with that boy again. But Fiddle turned back willingly enough.

They had not gone far, when a figure brushed past them and then another followed closely. The first was Emerson being chased by a heavy, clumsy-looking boy in overalls. They were turning out into the tall grass. Curious, Fiddle followed. Desty called to her to come back, and tried to catch her.

Just then Emerson fell. He was trying desperately to get up, when the big boy leaped on him, straddling him.

The grass hid them from the nearest campers, but she and Fiddle were close enough to see Emerson get pummeled unmercifully.

"Take that, you smart monkey, and don't go calling folks names no more," the big boy said and punched Emerson full on the nose.

When Desty saw the blood spurt, she felt sick. Emerson's hands flailed wildly but he could not protect himself. She did not like him, but she did not want to see him get half killed.

"Stop it, stop it!" She flew at the big boy, pulling at his overall straps. It was like trying to move a mountain. Fiddle joined her, catching the big boy's collar and tugging hard. "Let him go," they both screamed.

As he began to choke from the tightening collar, the big boy stopped punching Emerson. Then he turned on them as though he intended to give them the same kind of beating.

Fiddle backed away quickly. "Don't you — don't you come — near us, you — you —"

Desty was so frightened, she felt she could not move. She scarcely heard the man's voice calling from the nearest wagon, "What's going on over there?"

None of them answered, but the big boy turned away and hurried off. She was almost limp with relief as she watched his burly back disappear into the shadows.

Emerson still lay on the ground, sniveling. "Come on, get up!" Fiddle said. They each took an arm and pulled him to his feet. He was still crying when a woman came towards them. With the campfires behind her, they could not see her face beneath her sunbonnet, but they recognized her shuffling steps. It was Emerson's mother.

"What's happened?" she asked quickly. Then she touched the blood on his torn shirt and smeared across his cheek. "Who did this to you?"

Emerson kept right on crying. "I don't know his name. The big baboon —"

"There you go calling names again," Fiddle said.

The woman turned angrily to Fiddle. "Oh, it's you again."

Emerson broke in quickly. "They helped me, Maw. He liked to kill me if they didn't."

Well, at least he was fair enough to give them credit, Desty thought. She could not dislike him so much after that.

Dabbing at his face with her handkerchief, his mother said, without even glancing at her and Fiddle, "I'm thanking you for helping him." Then she put her arm around Emerson's shoulders and led him toward their campsite.

Watching them go, Desty thought they looked awfully lonely and pitiful. Did Emerson have a father, or were there just he and his mother making the Run in this wild, noisy land rush?

She had always hated violence. It made her stomach feel all queasy to see someone hit another. She was glad she was not a boy. She was afraid she would not make a very good one. But how much violence would the Strip hold before it was really a civilized place?

Uncle Gus's stories came back to her. Gun fights, fist fights. Mama always tried to shoo her and Fiddle out to play when he told those stories, along with the times he used "strong talk." But Desty heard most of them anyway.

Now she and Fiddle went slowly back to the wagon. Papa had lit the lantern and set it on the propped-up tailgate.

Mama looked at them sternly. "You should have stayed close by, instead of wandering off like that. Papa was just about to look for you."

When Fiddle blurted out about Emerson, Mama's lips tightened more. But when she heard the whole story, she . said she was glad they were of some help.

It had been a long, tiresome day. Desty would have been thankful to go right to sleep as soon as she lay down. But she could not. Neither could she shut out the thought that this was their last night in Kansas.

Finally she dozed off, but she kept waking up. There was scarcely any let-up in the noise and confusion of the last night on the line. It seemed that every time a horse stomped, or a dog barked or a man laughed, she heard the sound.

And each time she woke up she thought, tomorrow is the day. There is no going back now. Papa will make the Run, and before tomorrow night we will be living in the Cherokee Strip.

# Chapter Eight

## "Look at all the people!"

The first sounds Desty heard next morning were the voices of Burt and Jason telling Mama over again what went on at the border booth.

The boys must have gotten up early, because the hour was just past sunrise. She parted the canvas at the back of the wagon and saw Papa lounging on a patch of grass. He lay on his side, his elbow on the grass and his hand supporting his head. He did not say anything, just smiled and nodded and puffed on his pipe.

Mama was frying the cornmeal mush.

"I wouldn't want to be a sooner squatting on the quarter-section that that big bearded fellow in front of us picked," Jason said, wagging his head. "Golly, Mama, he was as big as a mountain."

Mama laughed. "Such exaggeration!"

"But he was, wasn't he, Papa?"

Papa nodded. "He was just about the biggest man I ever saw. Said his name was Pierre Chaison, a French portager from Canada. He just became a citizen last year."

Jason gestured eagerly. "And how about that man from Louisiana? He had his slave with him."

Papa corrected him. "No, Jason, not his slave — his servant."

"Well, the way he ordered him around, it sounded as if he were his slave."

Burt waved disgustedly at Jason's argument. "Slavery was done away with during the War Between the States."

Jason would not let the matter lie. "Well, it didn't sound that way. 'Boy, hold that horse still. Boy, get me a fresh *see*gar out of my saddle bag'!" He mimicked the man by puckering his lips, tilting his face, and flicking an imaginary ash from an imaginary cigar in his right hand. He hooked the thumb of the other into his suspender strap and strutted back and forth pompously.

He looked so funny, Desty had to laugh. Mama looked quickly towards the wagon. She smiled. "It's good to hear you laugh, Desty. Wake Fiddle and come to breakfast."

A short while later, Papa looked around at them all eating eagerly. "There's something about eating out under the sky that makes appetites big." He nodded toward Fiddle who was pouring a flood of syrup over her fried mush.

Mama looked at her with wide eyes. "Not so much

syrup, Fiddle. Our supplies will last no time at all if we all do that."

Fiddle seemed surprised for a moment, then as Desty reached for the syrup pitcher, Fiddle tilted her own plate over Desty's. "There, you have half now, just the same as me."

"As I," Mama corrected her. Then added, nodding, "That's better."

While Desty and Fiddle helped Mama clean up after breakfast, Papa and the boys repacked the wagon and took care of the horses and cow. Then they saw to it that the wheels of the wagon and buckboard were well-greased once more. And they checked the straps and ropes holding their supplies and belonging.

Several rough-looking men with shoulder-length matted hair and coarse clothing sauntered by. They waved to Papa and stopped to talk for a moment. Their speech was as rough as their appearance and they peppered their remarks with swear words. They glanced at Mama and said, "Beg pardon, Ma'am."

Mama quickly told Fiddle and Desty to take a little walk. That might work all right at home, Desty thought, but down here they heard the same thing a little farther on. There were so many men all keyed up about the Run, all trying to out-talk each other, that their voices grew loud and before long they were using coarse language. Then, shamefacedly, one or two of them would turn and apologize to any woman nearby. But they seemed to forget as soon as their conversation started again.

Fiddle giggled. "I wonder how far we'll have to go to get away from strong talk, clear back to our old house?"

Desty did not answer. She disliked any mention of the old house because the homesick feeling could come so quickly. It would be good to be in a house again, even a strange one. No matter what kind of a place they would have in the Strip, she was sure Mama would have it fixed up like home soon after they arrived. That thought made her feel better.

Walking along with Fiddle she wondered what Aunt Bessie would be doing now. Maybe washing clothes, churning butter, doing dishes or maybe ironing; the same chores that Mama had always done.

Fiddle turned around. "Come on, let's go back. We can't get away from strong talk anyhow." Fiddle giggled again, and Desty felt ashamed for her. After all, those words were not fit for a girl's ears, Mama said, and were not to be laughed at. But Fiddle's giggle was so contagious, she had to grin in spite of herself.

The morning grew hot and humid and the inside of the wagon was awfully uncomfortable. To get out of the sun, they hugged the shade cast by the wagon, but even that spot was not very cool.

Finally Mama and Desty and Fiddle took a walk to a small clump of bushes and trees. There in the shade some other ladies and girls sat resting.

One small, dark-haired lady with a slender figure and tiny hands and feet, smiled at Mama. "I'm Amy Jardine. This is my daughter, Claudette." Claudette was tiny like her mother but her eyes were blue and her hair was fair and curly. She reminded Desty of Marietta. And when Claudette said, "How do you do, Ma'am," to Mama, her quiet voice and daintiness made her seem even more like Marietta.

Desty liked her right away. She hoped she was not being disloyal to Marietta. It was so good to find someone different from all the loud, rowdy children they had seen on the trip.

Mama invited the Jardines to visit them after they were settled. Would all the folks inviting each other to their future homes really visit each other, Desty wondered. She doubted that they would even find each other. But she knew she would be disappointed if Claudette and her family did not come.

Walking back to their wagon, Fiddle asked Mama: "How are Claudette and her mother going to make the Run?"

"Claudette's father will ride a saddle horse and then come back for them. Mrs. Jardine's health is poorly."

Desty felt sorry for Mrs. Jardine. Living out in the open was difficult enough without feeling poorly. Then she realized something she had not noticed before. "Mama, why are there no old folks making the Run? Granny Buckskin is the oldest one we saw."

Fiddle disagreed. "How about the two old men who talked to Papa yesterday? They had hardly any teeth."

Mama nodded. "There are some hardy ones. But the land rush is a race. You have to be strong enough to keep up."

Papa was waiting for them at the wagon. "The boys and I scouted along the line. We have the buckboard in as good a place as any. The boys are staying with it now. We better move the wagon up a little closer behind it."

The ride was short, but slow and boring, because Papa had to take care threading in and out between campsites scattered everywhere. Of all the folks she could see milling about, Desty knew the ones she would like to see most again were Granny Buckskin and the Jardine family.

Everyone seemed to be moving about now. Nothing stood still — men, women, boys, girls, little tots, dogs, cats, cows tied behind wagons. Even some chickens, which most likely had escaped from a flimsy cage, were darting about. It was getting closer to starting time, and all those to be in the Run wanted to be ready. And all those who were going to wait behind wanted to be as near as possible, so that they could see everything.

Desty thought it all looked like a giant beehive, but there was no order here as she had seen in the beehives Marietta's father used to keep. Bees never acted so mixed up and confused in their coming and going.

Again Fiddle was all excited. She was bouncing and humming in the wagon bed. Fiddle never could be calm about anything. Back home, when she used to rock on Mama's rocker, she flew back and forth so violently, swinging her feet up in the air with such force, that it was a wonder she did not go head over heels, chair and all.

When Papa pulled the wagon to a stop, Fiddle climbed out the back and dropped to the ground. "Jumping grasshoppers! Look at all the people," she shouted, as though she had not seen them before. She seemed happy just to be in the middle of all the commotion. Desty wondered if Fiddle could ever be happy alone.

Well, she did not have to worry about that out here. Now there was even less space around the wagon than farther back. Folks seemed jealous of every inch. The buckboard stood right at the line waiting for Champ and

Duke to be hitched to it. Crowded on either side were other buckboards, wagons and all other kinds of vehicles. Tethered in between were the saddle horses.

"Oh, I wish we all were going to be in the Run!" Fiddle exclaimed.

According to Papa's instructions, Desty and Fiddle and Mama would ride in the wagon with Jason. They were to pull out after the run had started and drive leisurely towards the Chisholm Trail and go south on it for about two hours. That would bring them somewhere close to the middle of the Strip.

They were to wait there. No matter where Papa and Burt staked a claim, it would be easier and quicker to find them at such a spot than to come all the way back to the starting line.

Out beyond the starting point there seemed to be nothing but blackened ground stretching in every direction — no grass, no flowers, nothing. She was going to hate it, Desty told herself. Even if she tried not to, she knew she was going to.

The smoky smell of the burned-over land and the odors of horse manure and perspiration were mixed with the clouds of dust stirred up by the crowd. The smell almost sickened her.

Fiddle was crouching down now against the wagon wheel in the scanty shade. She held her nose. "This place stinks."

Desty could not help correcting her. "Say 'smell'."

Mama always told them to say "smell" instead of "stink" and "shout" instead of "holler."

But Fiddle forgot more often than she remembered. "There you go, being crabby again," she pouted.

Fiddle had been calling her crabby ever since Papa had decided to make the Run. Maybe she was; she could not help it.

"You're always crabby," Fiddle repeated.

"I am not."

"You are, too," Fiddle insisted.

Mama looked over at them. "Girls, girls, whatever is the matter? Isn't there enough noise without you two quarreling?"

"Desty's nothing but a crabby crab." Fiddle spoke as loud as she could. Then she stomped off towards Papa and Burt at the buckboard, mumbling, "Might as well be alone as have a crabby sister."

Oh well, let her say it, Desty thought. Mama did not believe it. Mama understood.

About ten-thirty, Papa and the boys came back to the wagon, with Fiddle straggling along behind them. Mama made some coffee and fried salt pork and pancakes. It was earlier than they had ever eaten lunch before. Besides that, the excitement shortened everyone's appetite. Therefore, in an awfully short while Mama had everything cleared away and packed back in the wagon.

When Papa said that he and Burt better get back to the buckboard, they all went along. On the buckboard, Papa had lashed his saddle and a package of food — some bread, cheese, and apples and several canteens of water. Fastened tightly beneath the straps was their stake with their name, SHAWN, printed in big letters. The stake, with its white flag, would be planted on their claim.

Everything else that the buckboard had hauled down here had to be packed into the wagon, until it was jammed full. And it jangled and rattled outside where the plow, buckets, tub and water barrel were fastened. Now Star really had a load to haul; but he was a strong horse, and they would not have to hurry.

Again, for the hundredth time it seemed, Papa checked Champ and Duke and the buckboard. Men were mounting their saddle horses and others were climbing to the seats of their vehicles. One young man and his wife sat stiffly in a fancy surrey hitched to a dainty little mare.

Two places down from their buckboard, a highstrung black saddle horse with a white face reared up on his hind legs. Its rider finally quieted him, but Desty could see the muscles rippling nervously beneath the horse's shiny coat. It stomped its white-stockinged feet constantly in the churned-up dust.

Its rider was a steely-eyed man with a square jaw and hair as black as his horse's. His travel-stained shirt was tucked into brown trousers with fine white stripes. They seemed too fancy for a land rush.

Time was growing short. Everyone was tense, fidgeting, waiting. Papa gave Mama and Jason the same instructions he had given them often before. "Take it easy, let the dust die down a little and then pull out and go west a short distance, until you hit the Chisholm —"

Mama nodded, assuring him, "Yes, Jason and I and the girls will do fine. You don't have to worry about us. You and Burt take care of yourselves. We'll be all right."

Then Papa kissed Mama, shook hands with Jason, and patted her and Fiddle on their heads. That was his "goodby for a while" to them.

Back at the wagon they settled down for the longest wait of all, the last fifteen minutes before the starting signal.

The anxiety had grown so tight, Jason said you could hear people squeak when they breathed. The sun was glaring down and Desty's underclothes stuck to her damp body. Her arms itched with the heat and dust, and there was black dirt under her fingernails from scratching. How good a bath would feel, or a few minutes wading in their little pond beneath the willows back home.

"Drinking water, drinking water," called a lanky young man in a battered wide-brimmed hat. He had several canteens hanging from straps slung over his shoulder and was selling water by the dipperful. One man paid him a coin that looked like a silver dollar.

Water seemed to be about the most outlandish thing to buy that she had ever heard of. But Papa had often said, "No matter what it is that's scarce, it will bring a good price." By now water was plenty scarce, especially among those folks who had been camping on the line for days, some even for weeks.

She wondered if there would be water on Papa's claim, or if they would have to haul it for a time, as Papa once said. To be without water at your own home must be a terrible thing. But she did not want to think of that now.

Instead, she thought of Granny Buckskin. She hoped Granny would get a good place on the train and stake a good claim. She hoped Claudette's family would, too. Then she thought of Marietta, and wondered if she would ever see her again. She thought of Aunt Bessie and Uncle Luke. But most of all, she thought how they were leaving Kansas today, now, too too soon.

## Chapter Nine
# The Run!

At five minutes before twelve, the noise thinned down. Jason sat stiffly holding the reins taut. He had his foot on the brake, too. By now Star was quite used to the crowds and commotion, but Jason did not want him to bolt when the signal was sounded.

Fiddle begged Mama to move over so that she could sit on the edge of the seat. Desty stood right behind them on a box in the wagon bed. From there she could see everything that was happening up ahead.

The quiet that settled over the throngs was eerie. Thousands of folks waited, perspiring under the glaring sun, with the hot wind swishing across the prairie full upon them.

The patrolling soldiers moved out of the way toward the end of the line. They raised their guns, ready to fire as soon as they heard the cannon signal.

At high noon the report sounded across the plains. Desty hoped she would never again have to hear and see such a din and melee as broke loose as that moment.

She could see Papa and Burt bounce on the buckboard seat, as Champ and Duke lurched forward when the reins slapped down on their backs. And then away across the uneven, burned-off, raw prairie, Papa and Burt raced to find their new home.

The shouting and cheering were ear-splitting. Before the curtain of dust shut off the view she saw several wagons lock wheels and jolt to a stop. She saw one rider topple as another sideswiped his horse. She saw the nervous black horse rear up again and dance in a circle like a circus horse. And all those waiting behind were screaming and tossing their hats in the air.

Even after the noise began to die down, Jason and Fiddle kept waving and calling, "Good luck, Papa! Good luck, Papa! Go it, Champ! Go it, Duke! Good luck!"

Then she saw Mama bow her head slightly and say, "God bless you, Henry, and good luck."

No matter how Desty herself felt about moving to a new, untried, empty land, now she wanted Papa to win. "Yes, Papa, good luck." She said it as though he were right there listening to her, because she meant it.

Suddenly new excitement broke loose. Out of the thick, hanging dust, came the nervous black horse, still rearing on its hind legs and swerving in a dash back from the line.

It seemed utterly uncontrollable now. Leaping and sunfishing, it arched its back exactly like an unbroken bronco that Desty had seen pictures of back home. Its head was twisted as its rider hauled on the reins in an effort to make it cross the line into the newly-opened territory.

Screams rose from the remaining camps where women and families were waiting behind for men who had ridden in the Run. Star was getting edgy too. Trying to calm him, Jason shouted, "Whoa, Star. Whoa, there."

The next moment the black horse was circling their wagon, wildly. It rolled its eyes in fright as it came up alongside them. "Whoa, whoa, there, boy," the rider yelled and raised his whip to lash it into a getaway gallop. But again it reared and swerved in close to Star, making the rider lurch violently in the saddle. And the whip came down hard across Star's back!

Star neighed loudly and jerked his head up and down. Then putting his strength into the harness he plunged forward. And off he galloped, wagon and all, in the wake of the Run into the Cherokee Strip!

Jason could not hold him. Mama caught the reins, too, and pulled with all her might, but that seemed to scare Star even more; all the while Jason and Fiddle kept up one long shout of "Whoa, Whoa!"

Behind them, Desty could hear the loud, frightened mooing of their cow being pulled along on her tether.

The wagon wheels seemed to find every prairie dog hole in the territory and every new rut made in the mad land rush. Desty thought the jouncing would kill her as the wagon careened along, swaying from side to side. No sooner would she grab hold of a box, a roll of bedding or Mama's rocking chair, than it would jolt across the wagon and she with it.

She could hear Jason's repeated frantic yells, "Whoa, Star! Whoa, Star!" But Star did not slacken. Suddenly she missed the cow's mooing, and knew that it had torn loose from the wagon.

Then there was one terrific jerk worse than all the others. The wagon leaned so far to one side that she feared it would turn over completely. Just as her arms flailed into the canvas near the rear of the wagon, she heard Fiddle's long, terrified scream.

Scrambling to the tailgate, she looked out into the blinding sunlight. For a moment she could see nothing. Then there was another terrible jolt and a shrill neigh from Star. And the wagon finally shuddered to a stop. It was then she saw Fiddle lying in a heap, absolutely still, about fifty yards away.

Climbing over the unopened tailgate, she could hear herself screaming, "Fiddle, Fiddle!" She fell as she dropped to the ground, and her palm was bruised on a sharp stone. Then gaining her feet, she raced madly back to Fiddle, stumbling, falling, running again.

She looked back over her shoulder and saw Mama and Jason following. "Oh, hurry, Mama. Hurry, hurry," she called.

Fiddle's face was white under the sooty streaks and the bleeding brush burns she must have gotten by skidding along after her fall. Her left arm looked odd, too. The bone at the elbow was making a huge bump and was almost sticking out through the skin. Desty felt sick to look at it. Then she realized that she was crying. She could taste the tears on her lips.

Over and over again she smoothed the matted, dusty hair back from Fiddle's forehead, pleading, "Fiddle, oh, Fiddle, wake up."

Maybe Fiddle was dead. Oh no, she can't be, she must not die, Desty told herself. She remembered all the times she was cross at Fiddle. "Oh, I'm so sorry. I'm so sorry. I didn't mean it." She found herself saying the words out loud. Then Mama reached them and gently pulled her upright.

Bending low, Mama touched the crooked arm very gently. "Oh, my poor, poor child. It's badly broken. Oh, my poor Fiddle." There was a little halt in Mama's voice. Catching her lower lip tightly in her teeth, she looked up toward the sky. Desty knew Mama was praying.

Then Mama sat down on the ground as close to Fiddle as she could. Bunching her skirt on her lap, she lifted Fiddle's head onto it, very slowly and tenderly.

To have Mama feel so terribly bad, made Desty forget her own crying, and she wiped her face on her sleeve. When she looked down again at Fiddle, she could have shouted with joy. Fiddle was opening her eyes; just a little squint at first, as she used to do sometimes when they played hide-and-seek. She must have felt pain in her arm then, because she glanced down quickly at it, and when she saw it she opened her eyes altogether, widely. "Mama, Mama, my arm! Will I die, Mama?"

Mama's face brightened. She smiled and shook her

head. "No, no, dear. It's just a broken arm. It will mend again. But does your back hurt, or your legs?" Fiddle shook her head. "Are you sure?"

Again, Fiddle shook her head. Mama motioned to Jason to pick Fiddle up. As he did so, he grunted in fun. "Gosh, you're heavy. Too many potatoes, or too much pie, either one."

Fiddle grinned a little at him and fastened her sweaty, grimy right arm tightly around his neck.

Desty helped Mama to her feet. "Will she be all right, Mama, really?"

"Oh, yes, I'm sure she will be if we can take care of her arm." But Mama looked worried as she shaded her eyes and glanced off across the prairie in all directions. "If we could only get hold of a doctor."

Mama's hair was falling out of the pins and was hanging down over her shoulder on one side. She coiled it, piled it on top of her head again and pinned it tightly. Then shaking her long skirt free of dust and bits of burned grass, she put her arm around Desty's shoulder and led her back to the wagon.

The sky was cloudless overhead and the sun seemed to grow hotter all the while. Desty wondered if any other landseekers had this much trouble so soon after the start. At the wagon, Jason put Fiddle down so that she could test her legs. She said she felt all right, except for her arm. She could stand quite well, but she winced when Mama wet a cloth and gently mopped the bruises on her face.

Jason went to unhitch Star. He came back almost immediately, looking oddly at them. "Something's wrong with Star, he's lame."

"We'll see to him just as soon as we settle Fiddle," Mama said.

They arranged some bedding beneath the rear of the wagon. Fiddle lay down with her injured arm resting on a pillow.

When they looked at Star, Desty could tell by Mama's face that something was dreadfully serious. Mama said, "I'm quite sure it's a broken leg. Oh, I do hope we can save him."

Save him! Did that mean they might have to destroy Star? Oh, she hoped Mama did not mean that. But now was no time to ask questions.

"You better go back to Caldwell," Mama told Jason. "See if you can find a doctor and bring him here. And hurry! Maybe he can tell us if there's anything we can do for Star, too."

Jason looked northwest. "We're about four or five miles from Caldwell, but I'll do my best," he said and started off immediately.

Once he was out of sight, the loneliness of the empty prairie seemed to wrap around her and Mama and Fiddle even more, Desty felt. Here and there a kettle or washboard or bottle lay, showing what a rough ride the land-seekers had and how the strappings on their belongings were strained. A short distance away a water barrel sat with its top hoop gone and its staves parted. Around its bottom was the darkening stain of the spilled water. She wondered what might have fallen off their own wagon, and where their cow had run off to.

Suddenly she heard a drumming sound. Shading her eyes she made out the figure of a horse and rider against the skyline off to the west.

Mama saw them too and waved and called for help.

But the rider only waved his hat in return. The horse swerved, reared up on its hind legs, and then leveling out, it headed south and ran like the wind. It was the nervous black horse that had caused all their trouble.

Fiddle was sleeping fitfully. Once in a while she stirred and moaned a little.

A short while later, another rider came by. He was going back toward Kansas. He dismounted and asked if they could spare him a dipperful of water. He had a big sandy mustache, and many lines at the sides of his eyes from much squinting into the bright sun of the plains. From his shirt pocket hung the string of a tobacco bag, and he wore a gun and holster.

As he drank, Mama asked him, "Couldn't you stake a claim? You're coming back so early."

"Didn't have the luck, Ma'am. I had one spotted before-hand. It was the nearest quarter-section right over there." He pointed southeast. "But someone beat me to it. Doesn't matter much, I had the sport of the Run anyhow."

He seemed to be telling the truth. He did not look much disturbed about the loss. Papa had said that some men might run for the sport of it. And others might stake claims to sell, or for others who did not want to make the Run themselves.

Replacing the dipper, Mama asked the stranger to look at Star's leg. He shook his head meaningfully. "No fixing that, Ma'am, he's finished."

"But my son has gone for the doctor, maybe he could help him." It was plain Mama wanted the stranger very much to say there was some hope, but he did not.

"Won't do you no good, Ma'am. I owned enough horses in my lifetime to see that."

Mama wrung her hands. The stranger looked at her sympathetically. "I can put him out of his misery for you, if you want." He touched his gun. So that was what Mama *did* mean, Desty thought. Star was going to be destroyed!

She ran over to Star and stood in front of his injured leg. "No, you can't kill him, you can't kill him. Mama, please don't let him."

"Sorry, little lady," the stranger said gently. "But he's suffering. A horse is no earthly good with a broken leg."

Mama reached out and caught her to her side. Desty heard the shot, but kept her face buried against Mama's skirt which still smelled of smoke and dust. It seemed that was all she smelled since they left home — dust, smoke, dirt. It was this horrible new land. Oh why, why had they come! She heard hoofbeats and looked up to see the stranger ride off.

The shot had wakened Fiddle and Mama went to comfort her.

Desty forced herself to look over at Star where he lay. Then she joined Mama. "What will Papa do now? How can start a livery stable? she asked. "Even Duke belongs to Uncle Luke."

"I don't know," Mama answered. "I just don't know."

Desty had hoped Mama might say they would have to return to Kansas. But she knew they could not give up yet. They had not even begun to homestead.

It was nearly sunset before Jason returned with a doctor. Mama ran to meet the light little buggy bouncing over the uneven ground towards them.

After a little pressing and probing, the doctor said that he would set Fiddle's arm.

Desty ran to the other side of the wagon and clapped her hands over her ears when Fiddle moaned, and she was sorry all over again for all the times she was nasty to Fiddle.

After the doctor left, she helped Mama get some supper ready, and then they settled down to wait through the long night out on the prairie.

# Chapter Ten

## Burt's Story

It was close to noon the next day when Desty heard Burt's loud shout to Papa. "Here they are, here they are!" he called,

Shading her eyes she could see him in the bright sunlight, riding Duke bareback, and waving his hand to Papa who was riding Champ a short distance to the south.

The ground throbbed with the horses' hoofbeats as they galloped up. Everyone talked at once. Papa and Burt were asking, and Mama, Fiddle, and Desty were telling. Jason just stood by with a great big grin spreading across his face.

Finally Papa said he could not understand a thing. Then he seemed to see, for the first time, Star lying beyond the wagon, and Fiddle's arm in a sling. "Nell, will you please tell me what went on here?"

Mama, by herself, explained what had happened. Papa shook his head in disbelief. He went over to take a better look at Star and came back, shaking head again. "Too bad, too bad," he murmured. Then he took off his hat, smoothed his bushy hair and replaced his hat.

"We searched all morning," he told Mama. "We asked every homesteader we came across, but no one had seen you. I was getting mighty worried." His face brightened a little then, as though he felt finding his family was all that mattered.

Poor Papa, Desty thought. But it was so good to have the whole family together again. Papa sat on Mama's rocking chair and held Fiddle on his lap. "So this little bird has a broken wing," he said, patting her shoulder gently. Fiddle settled back comfortably as they rocked slowly.

Meanwhile Burt was fidgeting, and Desty thought he was more excited than she had ever seen him. Finally, getting a chance, he began telling about the claim they had staked.

Papa grinned. "Go ahead, Burt, you tell them all about it. You earned the right."

Desty could picture the whole wild ride as Burt told it.

During the last five minutes before the signal shot, Burt kept telling himself that the land rush could not be as exciting as everyone said it would be. Nothing could be as wild and abandoned as some of the stories he had heard.

He watched Papa fidgeting with the reins. Papa sat easy and loose on the buckboard seat as though he were waiting to be launched bodily into the Run. His jaw muscles tightened and loosened and tightened again. Finally, he turned and said, "The last few seconds are always the longest."

Then the shot rang out. Burt was so tense from waiting that he actually bounced as the horses lurched forward. Then he grabbed hold of the seat and held on for dear life.

The stories *were* true, he thought, as he listened to Papa's loud Yahoo's and Giddaps. It seemed the whole world had gone mad. The dust rose in a sudden cloud like the smoke of an explosion, and the line surged forward in one violent movement.

When he felt the buckboard rolling steadily, he clung tightly to the seat with one hand and clapped the other on Papa's shoulder. "Good luck, Papa."

"Thanks, son. Come on, Champ. Giddap, Duke." Papa did not turn his head the slightest bit, but kept watching for his chance to veer off to the west towards the Chisholm Trail.

Once they came dangerously close to locking wheels with a wagon, but soon all the heavier vehicles were dropping behind. Saddle horses were leading the race, buckboards came second. Therefore, Papa had a pretty good chance of getting a choice claim.

After a short while the crowd had thinned out and Papa turned southwest. A little later the buckboard rolled onto the beaten track of the Chisholm Trail. Gosh, Burt thought, how much better it was than the uneven, chopped up prairie. They thundered south for about fifteen miles, he guessed, then Papa turned west once more.

Now they would have to watch for markers, which were on mounds of earth or stone slabs bearing the markings of the quarter-sections. They were beginning to see flags fluttering on claims already staked. They sped past one marker where three men were standing about haloing and pointing to a fourth untaken place on the marker. Saddle-horses were standing nearby.

Papa grinned and waved back. "Only horseback riders got here ahead of us," he told Burt. "We're doing all right."

"There's still one quarter-section there unclaimed," Burt shouted above the drumming the horses' hoofbeats.

"I know, but we'll take our chances on the next section," Papa said, again not moving his head.

They dropped down off a level stretch into a dry draw and followed it about a mile, to where it flattened out a little. There they found it easy to get the buckboard up over the bank without any fear of upsetting.

A little farther on, Papa rose up a little from the seat and nodded towards a marker. A short distance from it in three directions, flags fluttered. They found three stakes, and again the fourth quarter-section seemed unclaimed. Beyond could be seen a gentle grass-covered swell. This spot, like many places they had passed, had not been burned over.

Papa called "Whoa, Whoa!" and pulled hard on the reins. Before the buckboard fully stopped, both he and Burt leaped to the ground. Yanking the stake from under the strappings, Papa planted their flag, down through the tangled grass roots into the reddish earth. Going back to the marker he noted the number of his claim. Then looking at Burt, he shouted with great laughter and happiness in his voice: "The Shawn Acres, my boy, the Shawn Acres!"

Papa had not called him "boy" for a long time. It

seemed that in his joy, Papa forgot that he was not just
a young boy any more. But he couldn't get riled up at
Papa's slip of the tongue at a time like this.

Instead he held out his hand, very man-fashion, and
said. "You made it, Papa."

Papa shook hands vigorously, laughing and nodding.
Then Papa's face grew sober and he put his hands on
Burt's shoulders.

"No, Burt, *we* made it! You and I and Mama and
Jason and the girls, *we* made it." Then he gazed around
at the lush high grass waving in the sweeping wind, and
dropping his hands, he looked upward as though he were
giving thanks for the good fortune he had this day.

After a moment he reached for a canteen. "We're pretty close to the Salt Fork, I'd say." He meant the Salt Fork
branch of the Arkansas river. "Let's drink to it."

Burt had to grin as he took the canteen. The water was
luke warm, but no water ever tasted so good. "Oh, I nearly forgot," he said, fishing through the knapsack. He held
up two carrots. "I packed these for this occasion, a re-
ward for Duke and one for Champ."

They led the horses and buckboard farther back onto
the claim. When they topped the grassy swell, they saw
the land drop gently down towards a clump of cottonwoods and a fringe of bushes along a little gully. Papa
said there might be a stream. Leaving the horses, they
went to investigate. Sure enough, there was a stream,
quite narrow and low, but nevertheless a stream. A tangle
of weeds grew along its bank between the cottonwoods
and bushes.

Papa again surveyed his surroundings. "A wonderful
piece of land, the most wonderful on God's earth. Only

things missing are big trees, but we'll plant some here and there, and in no time at all we'll have plenty."

Burt pointed to the narrow stream of water in the creek bed. "That isn't much water, is it?"

Papa nodded, but did not seem bothered. "It's been a dry season, terribly dry. Lots of other creeks are altogether dried up."

Well, that was true, but right then Burt wished it were deep enough to dive into and swim around in for the rest of the day. His damp shirt stuck to his skin and his face felt like a clay mask. He could still feel the grit between his teeth despite the drink he had taken from the canteen.

Then he took a good look at Papa. Papa's face was smeared with the reddish dust from the trail and the black soot from burned-over areas. His teeth were so white against the grime that they looked like a jack-o-lantern smile. Burt could not help laughing.

"Your face looks like you just came from a war dance," he told Papa.

Papa laughed too. "You should see yourself!"

They unhitched the horses and led them down to the creek.

Handing Burt the reins, Papa said, "I think they're cooled off enough, but don't let them drink too much anyhow."

Then Papa filled his pipe and crossed the creek. He said he wanted to browse around a little on the rest of their land.

The slurp-slurp of the horses' thirsty drinking was suddenly cut by Papa's call. "Burt, come here a minute! Burt!"

Twisting the reins around one of the slender trees, Burt

leaped across the stream, and waded through the weeds and high grass for about fifty yards. There he saw Papa pointing silently to a stake and white flag.

"Do you mean someone beat us to this quarter section?" he asked Papa.

Papa's face had a strained look. "Seems like it, but I don't know. Let's look around."

Just ahead of them the land rose to a small hill, which they topped. Going down its other side, they almost stumbled over a form lying on the grass. It was a lanky, young man with stringy straw-colored hair, a sunburned face and large knuckled hands. At first they thought he was sleeping, but slowly he turned over on his side and looked up at them.

"I was a'wondering just when you'd find out that you're too late for this here spot," he said, chewing on a grass stem.

Papa looked flabbergasted, unable to speak. Rushing across the prairie on the buckboard they had seen no one make for this particular claim from any direction. He couldn't have come in from the western line because that was much farther away than the northern or eastern starting points. Still, he could have come straight down from the Kansas border and beaten them. If that was the case they would have to go on looking for an unclaimed place.

Out along the horizon, Burt could see puffs of dust and the forms of other landseekers drawing close, but he could not help feeling certain that he and Papa were the first from the line to claim *this* spot.

Papa was still staring at the young stranger. "Where's your horse? You couldn't have beat us here on foot, you know."

"Right over there." The stranger pointed. Sure enough, down from the rise and around the foot of it to the right, partially hidden by a scrubby bush, they found his horse.

"When did you get here?" Papa called.

"Just a few minutes before you did. Came from that way." The stranger waved his hand to the northwest.

Burt followed Papa as he strode towards the horse, with steps full of purpose. It was an old horse, more like a work horse than a runner. Silently, Papa looked at it as though he were listening for something. Then he touched its side, rubbed his thumb and forefinger together, smelled them. His face grew red with anger as he walked back to the lanky stranger. The stranger quickly got to his feet.

"You dirty sooner," Papa said, grabbing him by his shirtfront. "Get off this section, before I haul you into the land office and turn you over to the authorities." With a shoving motion Papa let go of the shirtfront.

The stranger almost fell over, then reached down for his battered hat on the grass. "I staked here first. You got no call to jump my claim." There was a shakiness in his voice, and all his cockiness was gone. He backed off.

Papa advanced on him again. "Don't call me a claim jumper. I know a hard run horse from one that's lathered with soap to make him look spent. Yours isn't even breathing hard."

The stranger darted towards his horse. Papa held up a warning finger. "And don't try to file on this quarter-section, because I'm heading right for the land office and if I see you there, you'll have plenty of trouble on your hands."

The stranger had scarcely mounted and spurred his horse away, before Papa rushed back to the buckboard for his saddle. Burt grabbed the horses' reins from the tree

and followed him. Throwing the saddle on Champ, Papa prepared to leave immediately.

Although Burt had heard plenty about "sooners," he never expected to see one. "Can he really file ahead of you and get this quarter section?" he asked Papa.

"Yes, and then I'd have to contest it. But maybe I scared him off. Champ is too tired to beat a fresh horse, but I must try."

Then Papa straightened, and putting his two hands on his back, he pressed it hard. Burt knew it hurt him and riding would make it worse.

"But your back will bother you. How far is it to the land office?"

"Oh," Papa guessed, "we're about twenty miles or more north of Enid."

It was after two o'clock and with Champ tired from the Run, and maybe a wait at the land office, it would be late evening before Papa could possibly return. But he had to go. Most likely, Mama, Jason and the girls would soon be reaching the place they were to wait.

It had been Papa's intention to go back to the trail to find them and lead them to the claim right away. Then he would file the next day. Some homesteaders would wait even longer than that. But the sooner changed Papa's mind in a hurry.

Papa checked Champ's cinch strap and turned to Burt. "I hope Mama won't worry too much, but if you leave here to find them, there's no telling how many more will try to stake here." He emptied his pipe and tucked it into his pocket. "Most folks are honest, though, and will go on once they see our flag."

Taking an apple from the knapsack, Papa tossed the sack to Burt. "Have a bite to eat, and take a rest." He mounted Champ and added, thoughtfully, "Mama won't be traveling very fast anyhow, and she'll know enough not to go too far south. Most likely she and Jason will set up camp right along the trail. We'll find them first thing in the morning." Taking a huge bite of his apple, Papa gave Burt a little salute and rode off.

Suddenly, Burt felt very lonely, with the rush of the Run all over with and the open spaces all around him. Although he often liked being alone, right then he missed company. He would be glad to see Mama, Jason and the girls.

First he hobbled Duke where he could graze. Then he made a sandwich of bread and cheese and washed it down with a drink of water. After a little rest, he gathered wood. He wanted to have it ready for a campfire when nighttime came along.

# Chapter
## Eleven
# Papa's Story

After Burt had finished his story of the Run, Desty sighed and was glad again that the family was back together.

But before Papa hitched Champ to the wagon to take them all to the claim, he told them what happened at the land office in Enid.

Once more Desty settled down to listen so she could picture what Papa experienced when he went to file their claim.

There were four land offices set up in the Cherokee Strip for filing claims and gaining title to the land. The nearest one to their quarter-section, of course, was Enid. The land office there was in a wooden L-shaped building, and was the land office and the post office together.

The assistant postmaster told Papa that he sat on the roof and saw the first homesteaders coming in to file. There was quite a line already formed by the time Papa got there. But Papa was pretty pleased with himself — he was the first to register of those who made the Run in a vehicle. All those ahead of him had made it on saddle horses.

But Papa had been awfully weary by the time he reached Enid. He had ridden steadily since leaving Burt on the claim. He was burdened, too, by anxiety, because he knew how awful it would be for the whole family if the sooner beat him to Enid and filed on the "Shawn Acres." Papa kept calling the claim that in his mind, and he prayed that it would belong to him, Mama, Burt, Jason and the girls.

But there he was in Enid at last. Standing in line he scanned the figures in front of him. There were farmers, store clerks, carpenters; and some of the others, by the cut of their clothes and by their talk, he judged were riverboat gamblers and saloon keepers.

Every time a smeared, streaked, tired face turned in his direction, he searched it for the features of the sooner. And he looked carefully at the back of every head for straw-colored hair.

Constantly he turned at the sound of approaching hoof-beats to see if the sooner might be bold enough to come in to the land office to file. But Papa never saw him again.

However, it was not until he reached the window, shoved through his certificate and stated the quarter-section he staked, that Papa drew a breath of relief. Then with the receipt in his pocket, he finally relaxed. But his back was aching badly.

He noticed, too, how relaxed all those who filed ahead of him were. Their tenseness was gone the same as his, and he exchanged a few words with some of them.

"Now we can rest our minds," he heard one fellow say to another. "I've been on pins and needles so long, it will feel good to set still."

There really was no place to "set" Papa thought, looking around. The land office was the only building in sight. He saw one red-faced man drink from a flask and he had to grin. Most likely the flask contained whiskey, but Papa told himself water was good enough for him.

Not until he drank from his canteen did he realize how thirsty he was. He wished the warmish water were cooler, but he was thankful just the same to have it.

It was then that he saw the woman, a plump little person in a buckskin jacket. She looked very familiar. Oh sure, he remembered — it was Granny Buckskin. She was standing close to the wall in the scanty shade of the building.

She seemed to be looking far across the prairie into the distance. Not until Papa stood right in front of her did she look at him.

"Mr. Shawn?"

Papa nodded.

Granny smiled, her small eyes sparkling pleasantly. "I wasn't sure right off. Everyone is more or less a stranger under this layer of dust and grime." She gestured toward her own face.

Papa shook hands with her and asked her if she had already filed.

"Oh yes," she answered with eagerness. "I got a fine spot in a townsite right along the railway. I've heard talk of the town being called Barryville, after a man named Oscar Barry."

"Well, you're mighty lucky," Papa said. "I suppose there was an awful crush on the train."

Granny nodded. "Yes, there was. At first the men were very considerate of me. But as the excitement grew, I was jostled about a bit." She patted Papa's arm. "And I have the space you wanted to rent if you still want it."

Papa assured her he would. Then he looked around. "How did you get here to Enid?"

"A fellow-townsman." Granny pointed to one of a group of men talking together earnestly a short distance away. "His son followed him in the Run with a wagon. They were kind enough to give me a ride." Then she added. "Now, tell me about the claim you staked. Where is it located?"

Papa explained where the claim lay.

Granny nodded again. "That should be about six miles west of the Barryville townsite."

Papa shook hands with her then, and said he would be in town to see her as soon as the family were settled on the claim. "In case it takes us longer than you to get settled, just come on out to the claim and visit with us. Nell and the children will be more than glad to see you."

The afternoon had worn away by the time Papa mounted and headed back towards the claim. He rode very slowly now, since Champ was tired. On the way many riders and wagon drivers, families and lone homesteaders hailed him.

"Good luck," he shouted to all of those he met who were hurrying towards Enid to file their claims. He found it easy to smile, tired as he was, because of the title paper in his pocket.

Twilight came on softly but still the wind swished across the prairie without letting up. He pushed his thick black hair back under his hat more than once and placed the hat firmly on his head. As did so he could feel the moist sweatband on his forehead. It would be good to get back, and go to bed in the coolness of the night.

But what about Mama, Jason and the girls. With the anxiety of filing the claim over with, he began to worry about them. Since he had told them to wait near the trail, they certainly would not be hunting for him and Burt. He had been so sure he would have been going back for them before now. Confound that sooner! Oh well, Mama and Jason would probably be setting up camp right this minute.

It sure was a long day. But he was coming to the end of his ride. It was good to get back to the claim. He could see the outline of the buckboard in the gloom. Nearby, the glimmer of a small fire welcomed him.

Burt jumped up and came forward to meet him. "Did you get there ahead of the sooner, Papa, did you?"

Dismounting slowly, Papa took off his hat and hit it against his thigh to beat the dust out of it. "Yes, I sure did," he laughed. "I don't know why I got so anxious about him. He's probably still running."

Burt spread a blanket near the fire and Papa promptly stretched out on it. Then Burt got the knapsack and made Papa a sandwich and handed him a canteen.

They lay for a long while looking up into the night sky all set with bright twinkling stars. They talked about where they would put the house, where they would plant corn, what kind of fence they would use around Mama's dooryard garden.

"I wonder where we should put —" Papa began to ask about the chicken coop, when he heard a faint snore. Burt had fallen asleep. With a little chuckle, Papa rolled over on his side. He hoped that by morning the ache would leave his back.

## Chapter Twelve

# The Sod Turners

When Papa finished his story about filing the claim at the land office, Desty smiled. Yes, indeed, it was wonderful to have the whole family back together.

But even though it seemed that Papa was over the shock of Star's death and the loss of their cow, his face grew grave when he spoke of it. He told Mama not to worry, they would make out well somehow. Then he went on talking about the fine claim he and Burt had staked.

Desty felt a little twinge. Now they would have to go homesteading. If only Papa had missed out on staking a claim — but she could not want Papa to have bad luck.

When everything was ready, Papa gave Champ a pat on the rump and climbed up onto the wagon seat. Burt was going to ride Duke. Inside the wagon Mama had fixed the bedding so that Fiddle could lie down comfortably. Desty sat at the rear of the wagon so that she could look out the back.

They had scarcely started when she saw something moving slowly in the distance slightly to the east of the wagon. It was an animal walking in a lumbering fashion. Maybe it was an injured horse. Its head hung low. She thought of poor Star and missed him. No, it was not a horse, it was a —.

She sat bolt upright and looked again. "Oh, Papa, stop, stop!" she called, leaning on the tailgate and pointing. "Papa, stop, there's our cow!"

So it was. Mama's face was shining, as she climbed down off the seat. Desty knew she had been worrying about where they would get milk, and how expensive it would be to buy all they would need.

Burt immediately spurred Duke in the direction of the cow.

Fiddle had crawled to the back of the wagon, holding her injured arm as far in front of her as she could to protect it. "Jumping grasshoppers!" she shouted. "Burt's a cowboy!"

Jason was standing nearby, scratching his head. "That cow's a puzzle. I tramped all over last evening and couldn't find a trace of her."

There was a reason, Desty thought. "It was dark, and the cow's black," she said without meaning to be funny. But Fiddle laughed out loud.

Jason laughed too. "Well, aren't you the smart one!"

He made believe he was coming after Desty. His teasing gave her a warm feeling.

Since the cow had been absent so long, she needed milking, so Mama promptly milked her.

Then with the cow tied securely to the rear of the wagon, they started off again. It was not as boring a ride as Desty had expected. Papa hummed on and off, pointing out in between something they could look at.

He called attention to a fine chestnut race horse lying near the Chisholm trail. "That poor horse was ridden to death."

Then he waved toward a broken water barrel. "Somebody's going to be awfully thirsty."

At the loud cluck-cluck of a lone lost chicken skittering across the prairie, he said, "That reminds me, don't forget to feed our chickens, even if they're living in crates."

"Oh, Papa," Fiddle told him, "we didn't forget. The poor things would be starved by now, if we had."

Jason laughed again and looked back into the wagon. "Boy, those two little redheaded girls are sure smart this morning," he teased.

The first things Desty liked when the wagon rolled onto the claim were the few cottonwood trees and the fringe of bushes along the creek. Water and trees, they had; not tall, massive trees, or abundant water, but they had them just the same.

Papa was so proud as he showed them around that he seemed as though he would burst. Burt showed them where the sooner had waited for him and Papa. "Lying right there, like he owned the whole Cherokee Strip."

"Here's where we'll put the house, the permanent one," Papa said, walking to a spot not far from the stream.

"We'll have to build a soddy first, of course, to live in until the big house is finished." He pointed a place a little farther along the stream. "That's where we'll put the soddy."

"Are we going to build the sod house today?" Fiddle asked. She was back to her old self again, inquisitive and ready for any kind of action.

"Yes, we'll start," Papa answered, looking at her arm in the sling. "But I know somebody who will have to do more watching than building." He patted her head.

Mama prepared a quick lunch for them and Papa immediately took the plow down from where it was strapped to the side of the wagon.

He plowed strips of sod about fifteen inches wide. Burt and Jason took the spade and axe and chopped the strips into pieces about thirty inches long and four inches thick. The longer Desty looked at the piles of sod, the harder it was to believe that she was going to live in a house made of them.

Fiddle seemed to be everywhere at once. Since she could not really do anything, she ran restlessly from the boys to Papa to Mama, watching everything. Her face still looked sore from the brushburns.

Mama must have thought so too. "The sun is rather hot. Maybe you should have a bit more salve on your face." She handed the little round box to Desty. "You put it on for her, dear, but touch the sore lightly."

Even while Desty was applying the salve, Fiddle could not keep silent. "Living in a sod house will be like living in the ground. I'm going to feel like a prairie dog."

Desty had to laugh. "Oh, I don't care, just so we have a house." Just so we get inside away from all this open

space, she thought. She knew then she would feel more at ease, maybe even a little at home.

Papa stopped plowing to drive stakes for the corners of the house. He said the house would be about twenty feet wide and thirty feet long. Later he was going to put down a wooden floor and a wooden partition through the middle of it to make two rooms.

"We'll get the wood just as soon as the lumber yard opens up in Barryville," he said wiping his forehead on his sleeve.

It seemed funny to talk about a town that was not even there yesterday. Maybe it was not even all there yet today, or would not be for weeks. But Papa assured them it would be complete very soon.

Knowing that Granny Buckskin was going to live in that town and would come out to visit them and would let them visit her, was so, so comforting.

After Papa and the boys had a big supply of sod cut and ready, they started to lay them around the stakes at the corners and then in straight lines for the sides of the house. They lay them grass side down like bricks, placing them firmly on top of one another so that the wall would not topple over. But it took time, and the afternoon wore away before they finished the four walls.

The roof was going to be made from poles, also covered with sod. Papa was even going to make the chimney from sod. "We'll mix earth with water to make a wet clay. Then we'll plaster the inside of it as we build it," he told the boys.

"We'll have to build a barn for the cow and horses too," Burt said. Papa agreed.

The Run was only yesterday, but Burt seemed so much more grown up, Desty thought. He was almost as much help to Papa as a grown man would be. She liked Burt when he talked and let you know what he was thinking. But it was hard to like him when he went around silent, without ever laughing or smiling.

Jason was the same as he always was. "Maybe we should build the barn first," he said, his eyes twinkling. "If it rains we could all crawl into the wagon, but how could we get Champ, and Duke and the cow into it?"

Fiddle nearly doubled over langhing. Then she stopped suddenly when she swung her right hand into her injured arm. Mama told her to take a little rest. Suppertime was drawing close, and Papa said he thought they had done enough for one day.

But twice during the next three days Papa and the boys had to dash off on the buckboard to help fight a grass fire. Many people were still camping or living in wagons, and some of them were careless with their open fires. The prairie grass was long, tangled and dry, and once the grass caught, it took a lot of fire-fighting to put it out. The wind swept on constantly and every hand that could be spared was needed.

Around their own place, Papa plowed a strip to protect them. The fire would stop at the freshly turned earth, if it burned in their direction.

Finally they had the house finished, and Papa and Burt took the wagon into Barryville to buy wood for the floor, window frames, and a door frame. Lumber was very much in demand, and they had to pay more for it than they had expected to.

Desty wished she could have gone to town with them, especially when they said they had seen Granny Buckskin. Granny said she was awfully sorry to hear about Star. But she told Papa not to feel too badly about not starting a livery stable. Down the narrow, rutted street from her place a big sign hung which read: "Livery Stable, Rigs for Hire." Granny said the owner had eight horses and three carriages for rent. He also had his own blacksmith.

"So you see," Papa told Mama, "I would have had some awfully steep competition."

"What does that mean," Fiddle wanted to know.

"That the other stable would get more business than I would." Papa tweaked her ear and called her nosy.

As Papa and the boys put the boards down side by side for the floor, Papa paused a moment. "I guess we were lucky to get enough for the floor. We'll divide the rooms with blankets until we can get wood for a partition."

Then while he and Burt and Jason went to work cutting more sod to start building the barn, Mama and Desty put their belongings into the house. Mama's rocking chair seemed to be the best link with back home, and it made the dark little room in the sod house seem cozy.

Mama hung sheets and burlap around to hide the earthen look, even though the boys had flattened the rough sod walls as well as they could with the flat of the spade. Then she placed the trunk against one wall and covered it with a checkered linen towel.

Standing back to look at it, she smiled. "As soon as Papa gets the windows in we'll make some curtains for them and it will look much better in here."

There was no door either at first. They would have to wait until Papa bought wood to make one, and glass for the windows. But when the table was put together and the stools and a new bench made, it seemed that the little soddy was well furnnished.

In the sleeping room, behind the hung blankets, Jason ran a piece of wire out through the sod and bent it outside so that it would not slip, and inside he bent the end to make a little hook. Then he announced proudly, "That's to hang your picture on." He meant their "Stable of Bethlehem" picture.

What a wonderful surprise, Desty thought. "Oh, thank you, Jason."

Fiddle thought so too. "That is where our bed will be," she indicated the place right beneath the hook. Desty immediately laid out their bedding.

Papa breathed easier when the barn was done. They finished the door and got glass for the windows and at last everything was settled — except for the partition. But that could wait.

"We'll have to dig a well later on. But we're lucky to have the stream, low as it is," Papa said. "Other folks had to start on a well first thing and haul water until they finished it." Lighting his pipe, he added, "The next thing we'll do is plant turnips. We'll have a crop for the winter."

Jason's face grew happy. He loved to work as a farmer, planting, reaping, cultivating. "I'll do it, Papa," he offered quick as a wink.

Papa grinned. "Sure, Jason, but Burt and I will help."

Desty was not overjoyed with the thought of turnips. She always picked them out of the mulligan stew when Mama made it. Mama did not scold her though, because she said everyone could have one dislike. And Desty could honestly say she was not picky about any other food.

But Mama was glad that they were putting in a turnip crop for winter. "We'll need all the food we can store away," she said.

Desty had seen how carefully she had rationed out the supplies lately.

Papa had lit his pipe and was seated on a stool with his back leaning against the sod wall.

Fiddle pulled another stool close to him. "Tell us a story about Kit Carson, Papa."

And Papa did. Not only about Kit Carson, but other frontiersmen whose names Desty had never heard before now. "They were all good men," Papa said. "They died with their boots on."

"What does that mean?" Fiddle asked, shifting on her stool.

"Oh, it means a man dies while doing his duty, or in readiness for it. It means he did not die in bed."

Was that why Papa never relaxed and wore his house slippers, Desty wondered, because he wanted to be always in readiness? She shuddered. She did not want Papa to die with his boots on. She corrected her thought — she did not want Papa to die at all.

# Chapter
# Thirteen
## The Jardines

It took three days to get the turnip crop planted, because
on each of those three days smoke was seen spiraling
skyward. Without hesitating, Papa and the boys hitched
up the horses to the buckboard and rode off in its direction.

But finally the turnips were in and Papa and the boys
dug the well. The grass around the dooryard was cut and
trampled down. Mama had her little vegetable garden
marked off and she planted her flower bulbs, irises and
tulips. She also transplanted a rose bush which she had
brought along from home, and she watered it carefully.
When it perked up and looked alive, she was very pleased.
"Someday we'll have a rambling rose and a honeysuckle
too," she promised.

The unfriendly, raw look of the soddy was beginning to disappear. A lived-in, cozy feeling filled it. But still Desty often thought that if for some good reason they should return to Kansas, she would be terribly, terribly happy.

After the well was finished, Papa said he had to start looking toward a livelihood.

"What's that?" Fiddle asked.

"Why, that means making a living," Papa explained.

"Well, isn't our homesteading and farming going to do that?"

"Yes," Papa answered. "But we were going to have a livery stable too, remember." Then he seemed to be talking to himself for a moment. "But with Star gone, there's no hope of that. Anyway I could never keep up with that other livery stable. But," he pushed his bushy hair under his hat and grinned, "I could still find some work hauling, I believe."

For the next several days, he and Burt went into Barryville and found hauling jobs. Sometimes, they hauled lumber out to homesteads for men who could not take all they ordered on one trip and did not want to spend time going back to town. Other times, they hauled crates of goods to business places. And sometimes they used Champ and Duke to help remove large rocks and tree stumps for clearing.

But more and more they helped to haul the belongings of homesteaders to the train depot in Barryville. This was more a favor than a job. Some of the homesteaders sold their wagons and horses to pay their fare and the shipping charges of their possessions. Some of them lost their wagons in fires. None of them had much money, and could only pay Papa very little.

But this was a sad job. Those homesteaders were leaving the Strip. Some of them had staked claims which were dry and windswept with no water. Wells had to be sunk too deep and they gave up. Some ran out of supplies and had scarcely any money left. They did not want to get stuck for the winter without either.

Still others found homesteading far from their liking and preferred life back where they came from. Then there were some who were moving into town to rent living quarters and become townspeople.

But mostly Papa and Burt hauled for the business places, the feed store, and furniture store, the lumber yard.

Once in a while, with some of the money they earned, Papa would buy a few pieces of lumber. He put up the wooden partition in the soddy, as he had planned, with a curtained doorway. After that he bought lumber little by little for the new house. "Every bit helps," he said. "Some day we'll have enough for the whole house, doors, windows, staircase — everything."

Desty found a lot of pleasure in dreaming of how their new house would be. It sounded so grand the way Papa told it. As she sat stitching hems for Mama in the lamplight, she would imagine she was in a fine sitting room sewing beside a lace-curtained window that reached from floor to ceiling. Then she would start thinking of their house in Kansas and missed it and hoped the new one would be just like it.

One day she and Fiddle found a lark's nest in the tall grass. Later, telling Papa, she said, "But the bird that flew away from it didn't look like a lark."

"That was a cowbird," Papa told her. "Cowbirds take over other birds' nests if they can."

"Just like sooners," Fiddle said, laughing. "They should be called be called 'Sooner Birds'."

The weeks had slipped into mid-October. Fiddle's arm had mended well, and she was not wearing a sling any more. Mama kept reminding her to exercise it so that it would regain its full strength. But Fiddle scarcely had to be told to do that. She was as lively as ever. She and Desty, now that the excitement of settling in was over, explored every inch of their claim.

But some days time hung heavy. Desty often wondered why some of the folks who had been so quick to promise to visit did not come around. The ones she was most disappointed in were Granny Buckskin and Claudette Jardine.

Mama tried to explain. "Well, Granny has a business to take care of, and a home to set up, too. It's twice as hard for her to get away as it is for us. And we haven't visited anyone either." Then she promised, "Before long we'll go into town to see her."

And of the Jardines they heard nothing, until one day Papa came home from town and said, "Burt and I met the fellow on the quarter section next to us on the northeast end. We saw him in town today and he told us his name was Jardine." Papa turned to Mama. "He said his wife and little girl met you."

"That's Claudette," Fiddle shouted. "Oh, Mama, could Desty and I go visit her, please, Mama."

"Yes, Mama, please," Desty pleaded too.

Mama put her two hands up in front of her, laughing. "Just a minute, you two. The afternoon is almost gone. And you still have to do your lessons. It's too late today, but tomorrow you may go, if you do your chores early enough." Mama always insisted that they both do sums and some reading and writing each day until a school could be built.

Desty was so happy she soared through her lessons that evening. And the next day too. She and Fiddle cleaned up their tasks so quickly, Mama had to inspect their work to see that they really did it.

It was the happiest day for Desty since they left Kansas. They were going to visit a friend. She thought of Marietta, and still considered her the very best friend of her life, but going to see Claudette made her so happy.

When Claudette saw them, her face shone with joy. But her small pointed features seemed narrower than before, as though she had to worry like a grown-up.

The Jardine soddy was smaller than the Shawns', but it was big enough for Claudette and her parents. A half-dug well could be seen about twenty feet from the doorway, but there was no garden like Mama's and the tall grass still was long and tangled around the house.

It did not look very much "lived-in" thought Desty. Then she remembered Mrs. Jardine's illness, and asked Claudette how she was.

Claudette's smile quickly faded. "Not so good. She coughs a lot more than she used to." Then Claudette smiled again. "But she would like to see you." She led them into the little soddy.

After a moment or two, when Desty's eyes grew used to the dimness, she realized there was only one small window. She guessed that Claudette's father was not as good a homesteader or builder as Papa; but then, Mr. Jardine had to do it all himself. Papa had the boys' help. On a bed along one side, she could see Mrs. Jardine lying down.

"Hello, Mrs. Jardine," Fiddle said immediately.

Desty remembered Mama's instructions. "Mama said to tell you she was asking for you."

Mrs. Jardine sat up slowly and drew the coverlet close around her. "That's very nice. Tell your mother I said thank you."

Then Mrs. Jardine motioned to Claudette and Desty could see how frail and pale her hands looked.

"Get the girls some lemonade." Her voice, too, was frail and whispery.

After a short while, Mrs. Jardine leaned back. "You girls go out and play and have a nice time. I'll just lie down for a while."

Claudette was overjoyed when Fiddle suggested looking for a lark's nest. They found one. Then they gathered some autumn leaves and Claudette fashioned a bouquet of them with some tall grass stems in between. It was very pretty.

"My mother likes pretty things," she told them, and immediately helped Desty make the same kind of bouquet for Mama.

The afternoon just flew, and before they knew it, she and Fiddle had to leave for home. Claudette promised to visit them as soon as her mother felt better.

"But don't wait for me to visit you," Claudette's voice sounded sort of hopeless. "Come to see me again soon."

Desty felt awfully sorry for Claudette, and she and Fiddle promised to come again a week from that day.

Desty tried to picture how it would be if Mama were so sick and again felt sorry for Claudette. But it was so good to have a friend nearby once again. Going to see Claudette would be almost like visiting Marietta. Maybe, Desty told herself, she would learn to like the Cherokee Strip sooner than she had expected.

But the following week, just the day before she and Fiddle were to visit Claudette, Papa brought the sad news.

"When Burt and I got to town this morning, guess who we saw," he said to Mama. "Jardine."

Desty was surprised. Claudette had told her and Fiddle that her father never went into town until the afternoon, when he was sure everything was done around the house and that her mother was able to rest.

"We're going to visit Claudette tomorrow, "Fiddle announced.

Papa looked at them rather oddly. "I'm afraid not," he said and puffed on his pipe a few times.

Desty sensed a strange feeling creeping over her. What would Papa say next?

And it was to her that Papa spoke. He took his pipe from his mouth and looked straight at her. "Because Mrs. Jardine got much worse. The doctor said she had to go to a hospital. So they are going back to where they came from." Papa walked to the door and looked out over the prairie reddened by the setting sun. "Burt and I hauled their things to the depot about noon. They used their own wagon for Mrs. Jardine. Just a bed in it for her and a chair for Claudette to sit with her. She's a pretty sick woman."

Desty ran through the curtained doorway into the sleeping room. Lying face down on her bed, she cried bitterly. Mama went to her and held her close. "You must not feel bad, dear."

"Oh, Mama why must we part with every friend we have?"

"I don't know, but you'll make other friends. Claudette's mother needed more care than she could get here, or she would never get well."

Desty wiped her eyes. She trusted Mama's words. "We didn't even say goodbye to her," she said, trying not to cry anymore.

Papa heard, and came to the curtained doorway. "Claudette told me to tell you she said goodbye and gave me this address. You can write to her."

He handed Desty a paper. She read the address: Independence, Missouri. How far away it sounded. If only Mama and Papa decided to move back to Kansas. Marietta was still there. But what was the use of thinking of that.

Mama pressed her hand. "Besides, there has been talk of a school being built soon. You will meet new friends there."

Fiddle had been standing nearby. "School!" She said the word as though it was something unheard of.

"Yes, school," Papa laughed. "Right after the beginning of the new year. You'll probably have classes come spring. You and Desty and Jason."

Jason sank down on a stool as if he were struck. "You mean I have to go to school!"

Burt came in from tending to Champ in time to hear Jason's remark. "Why not?" Burt's voice sounded smug. "I went until I was fourteen. You missed this term, so you'll have to go until you're fifteen, or maybe seventeen, or eighteen." He grinned at Jason's discouraged look.

Fiddle giggled, but Jason did not think Burt was funny. He stuck his tongue out and made a "Naa-ah" sound.

Mama had to smile, but she said, "That's enough teasing."

Desty knew Burt would let the matter rest there. He never talked very much on any subject. But she wished someone would talk more about school. It would be good to have pencils and paper and books again, and as Mama said, meet some new friends. Some of them were sure to be like Marietta and Claudette, at least a little bit.

But she would have to wait until the new year came around. And until then, there was Thanksgiving and then Christmas to look forward to. She resolved to think only nice cheerful thoughts so that she could push the sadness of losing Claudette out of her mind.

## Chapter Fourteen
# "My name is Blue Wing"

A great deal of the building was over now. The towns-people and the homesteaders were settling in for the coming winter. Most of those who were leaving the Strip were gone.

Little by little Papa's hauling work dwindled away. Lack of money also brought the building of their new house to a stop. By the middle of November their food supplies were awfully low and almost everything they needed had to be bought in town.

Desty wished she and Fiddle could walk to the store as they did back in Kansas. But now the boys usually went to town with Papa in the wagon.

Then one day when the sun was bright on the brown

dry grass, and the air was sparkling clear, Papa said, "How would you two young ladies like to go into town with me while the boys are harvesting the turnips?"

"Is Mama going too?" Fiddle asked.

"No," Mama answered quickly. "I have things to do. The boys will be here. I'll be all right."

Desty felt Mama did not care to go to town because she did not have the money to buy things they needed. But Mama smiled and told her and Fiddle to run and get ready.

As Desty put on her good shoes, she could feel them pinch. They were becoming too small. Fiddle's were too.

"I'll need new shoes soon," Fiddle announced. "These hurt."

Mama winced. "That's another thing to put on our list."

"What list?" Fiddle asked. Desty wished she would hush.

"Of things we need," Mama answered.

Papa was looking at Mama in a worried sort of way. "It seems like a long time since September, doesn't it?" He patted Mama's arm and puffed on his pipe. "But everything will be all right."

Papa always said everything will be all right. But what if things kept getting worse. Would Papa change his mind? The framework of their new house stood like a lonely, deserted silhouette against the sky. What if Papa could never finish it? They could not live in a soddy forever. What would they do?

Papa was calling for them to hurry. Mama kissed them goodbye and told them to have a good time.

The road to town was quite plain to see now. The high grass was flattened and there were wagon tracks to follow. They passed some fully built wooden houses, some houses only half completed and many soddies. In town, though, there was a good number of homes, some of two stories, all finished with porches and fences and everything. And many of the shops and stores had rooms above, or in back, where the owners lived.

And the town noises! After the quiet out on the homestead, the sounds of town were loud. There were rough shouts, tinny piano music, loud laughter, horses clip-clopping by, wagons rumbling past, conversation, jokes, and arguments. It was good to come to town, but now that she was here, Desty thought, all the sounds suddenly melted into one great big noise.

Papa took them to the general store owned by Mr. Rudolph Bingle. It was the first store in Barryville and Papa had been there before. Mr. Bingle had a lot of merchandise which he brought down from a store that had failed in Wichita. But business did not seem very good. They looked around until they were tired, while Papa talked to Mr. Bingle.

"It's that other store. Too much competition. Hardly sell anything since they opened," he told Papa. But Desty noticed the merchandise was dusty and lay in heaps on the counters. The shelves were half empty, and barrels and rakes and garden forks were shoved haphazardly against the wall.

"Hardly any business at all." Mr. Bingle said again. Then reaching for the candy jar, he handed Desty and Fiddle each a lemon-flavored stick. He had a wide, rugged face with many deep lines. But when he smiled all the lines turned upward making his face into a merry jack-o-lantern. The trouble was Mr. Bingle's smile was a very short one. The lines in his face turned down too quickly.

While he was talking, Papa was stacking some boxes and bottles on the end of the counter in a nice even display. Then he took off the other items that cluttered the counter, and mentioned that the display might attract customers. Looking farther, Papa told Mr. Bingle that the bolts of yard goods were getting too dusty lying flat on the shelves, that they would be better standing on end with just the edges showing.

Mr. Bingle said Papa had some right good store ideas, and if he ever wanted any help in the store he would remember Papa.

They were at the door ready to leave when Mr. Bingle asked, "Still doing any hauling?"

"Oh yes, if I get the chance. Doesn't seem to be much work at it right now though."

"Well, you might have some soon. My daughter's husband had a bad fall, broke his leg. They've had nothing but bad luck on that claim they staked. Now with this, they decided to give it up and move in here with me for a while."

"I'm sorry to hear about their bad luck," Papa said, "but I'd be happy to haul their things. When should I see them?"

"Tomorrow would be all right," Mr. Bingle answered. "Here, I'll mark down directions to their place."

Papa turned to the girls. "Well, we'll have to go now.

You want to see Granny Buckskin, don't you."

"Oh, yes," Desty said quickly. Now their trip to town would be perfect. The candy was delicious but seeing Granny again would be better.

On the way down the street, they came across a group of boys pushing a little halfbreed girl off the wooden sidewalk.

"Get out of our way, you little old Indian squaw," one boy said. He was freckled-faced, with straggly hair. His overalls were faded and his voice was familiar. Desty recognized Emerson.

"It's Emmy," Fiddle said loudly.

Emerson looked towards them, with a half-curious, half-afraid expression. When he saw who they were, his expression became surly. "Do you want a good punch —" he began, starting toward them. Then he saw Papa and backed away.

"Emerson has a girl, Emerson has a girl," one of the other boys chanted, and they began shoving him from one to the other. He fell and they pulled him up and shoved him again.

Papa stepped in. "Here now, let him alone. Three to one is not fair."

The others ran off and Emerson started in the opposite direction. He stopped for a moment and called over his shoulder, "Thanks, mister."

"One of these days, we won't be around to help him and he'll get himself killed," Fiddle said, between licks on her lemon stick.

Desty only half-heard her. The little Indian girl was still standing in the dusty street watching them.

Desty went towards her. "Hello." Breaking her candy in two, she handed the Indian girl a piece. "Here, take it, it's good."

The Indian girl stood absolutely still for a moment and then reached out and snatched the candy quickly. Her black eyes were wide and frightened. "Go on, eat it." Desty said, licking her own piece.

The Indian girl licked hers and a smile flashed across her face. Then soberly, she kept eating the candy.

Desty pointed to herself. "My name is Desty. This is Fiddle. What's your name?"

"My name is Blue Wing." She spoke in clear English and her voice was soft.

Fiddle asked, "How old are you?"

"Ten years old." She did not say ten summers or winters in the way Desty always thought Indians talked.

Up the street, Emerson was watching them. Then he started back. Blue Wing turned to go.

"No, don't go," Desty said.

Fiddle joined in. "He won't bother you. We won't let him."

Emerson stood about ten feet away. "I'm sorry I pushed you," he told Blue Wing, and then left quickly.

Once again Desty had to change her mind about liking Emerson. It seemed he always did something quite fair after he had acted badly. She wondered where he lived, and how he and his mother made the Run.

Papa led them on down the street, and they waved goodbye to Blue Wing. But when they reached Granny's door, they saw that she had followed them there.

"Do you live around here?" Desty asked her.

"Yes, here." Blue Wing pointed to Granny's and walked past them, pushed the door open and went right in. Surprised, they watched her thin little figure in the blue and white calico dress disappear inside.

Granny's voice reached them from the back of the place. "Oh, you're back. Did you see your mother?"

"No," Blue Wing answered. Desty was baffled. Blue Wing sounded as if she lived with Granny.

Papa stuck his head through the doorway and called, "She had a little trouble with some rough boys."

Granny almost ran to welcome them. "Come in, come in."

They had to enter through the laundry room which was a big room smelling of soap suds and wash water. There were three tubs in it, a stove and a copper boiler for heating water. Across one end, washlines were strung to hang laundry inside when it rained.

Granny led them through to her living quarters. In her kitchen, there were two chairs, a bench, a rough table, a cookstove, a cupboard, a little cot and a long shelf bracketed to the wall. On one side there was a door which Desty guessed led to a bedroom.

Granny pulled up the bench for them and then turned to Blue Wing. "I see you have met my friends."

Blue Wing nodded.

Then Granny explained that Blue Wing's mother worked for the Abernathys. "That's the biggest house in town, right down at the end of the street. It has a picket fence in front and high board fence at the sides and back. All white-washed, you can't miss it."

Then she told how the Abernathys had three children and did not allow Blue Wing around the house because the children were not to play with her. So when Blue Wing's mother had to stay overnight on weekdays, Blue Wing stayed at Granny's and slept on the little cot in the corner. On weekends she lived in a hut out on the prairie with her mother. It was an old cattlemen's hut and the homesteader who staked the claim where it stood rented it to them.

Blue Wing's dead father was a white man. Maybe that was why Granny felt so close to Blue Wing. Granny's daughter was a halfbreed too.

But Desty felt very sorry for Blue Wing. She must have had a lonely life. Yet, Desty felt happy, too, because Blue Wing lived with Granny, and hoped Blue Wing would become a friend. The little Indian girl, however, just stood to one side, as silent as a statue, until Granny went to the cupboard and motioned to her.

"Get some mugs out please, so you and the girls can have some milk and cookies." Granny turned to Papa. "Would you have some coffee, Mr. Shawn?"

While they were enjoying the snack, Granny had to hear all about Mama and the boys. She promised to come out and see them as soon as she could. The afternoon went too quickly.

All the way home, Desty thought of the nice things that happened, visiting the store, meeting Blue Wing, seeing Granny. The ride to the claim was over before she knew it, and Papa was helping them down in front of the soddy.

Fiddle ran into the soddy ahead of her and blurted out all about the happenings of their day to Mama. "And Mama we met an Indian girl, she lives with Granny and her name —"

Mama quickly hid something in the trunk and held up her hands. "Not so fast, Fiddle, not so fast."

Desty was glad Mama shushed her. She wanted to tell Mama about Blue Wing herself. "She is smaller than us and she has the blackest hair you ever saw, Mama, in long braids over her shoulders. Her name is Blue Wing."

Mama smiled. "What a lovely name."

"Do you think Granny would bring her out here sometime?" Desty asked.

"Oh, I'm sure she will. I'll ask her to." How wonderful Mama was.

But now it was Papa's turn to tell Mama his news. "The experience I got working in that drygoods store in Ohio, seemed to come back to me as soon as I handled Bingle's merchandise," he said. Desty had forgotten Papa worked in a store before. He never seemed to talk much about it. Papa went on. "And Bingle said if he ever needed help he would think of me. It would be nice to get a job there for the winter. Anyway, Burt and I have a hauling job tomorrow."

Mama smiled again. "That's fine."

"Yep," Papa said. Then he sort of jerked his head at Mama and asked her, "Did you start on — what you wanted to do?"

"Yes," was all Mama said.

What did she want to start, Desty wondered, and remembered Mama hiding something as they came in. But it had only looked like an old sweater of Papa's.

# Chapter
# Fifteen
# *Duke*

Papa and Burt set out early the next morning for Mr. Bingle's daughter's place. They took the wagon and Duke; Papa said Champ had done more than his share of the plowing and much of the hauling, too.

"I don't know when we'll be back," he told Mama. "I don't know how much stuff they'll want taken to town. Bingle lives over his store. The place isn't very big."

"It's a shame they couldn't keep their claim," Mama said, handing Papa a bag of sandwiches for lunch.

"Yes, it seems like half the folks who went through so much to get a claim are giving up before they're rightly started," Papa said.

"But you couldn't expect Mr. Bingle's daughter and her husband to stay with so much against them," Mama answered.

It was funny, Desty thought, Mama could understand other people giving up, but Mama herself would probably stay no matter how much trouble they had.

Papa and Burt climbed up to the wagon seat, waved and drove off.

When Papa was away, Desty missed him. At home he was always laughing and joking and singing silly little songs, as he worked around the claim.

But the day passed quickly. Mama sent her and Fiddle out to help Jason with the turnips for a while. They also did their household chores and their lessons. They fed the chickens, and played in the high grass and bushes down along the creek. They even walked all the way to a fringe of scrub oaks that bordered the claim west of theirs.

It was almost twilight before Papa and Burt returned. But Papa did not laugh and joke this evening. His eyes looked tired and very worried. Something must have gone awfully wrong.

Desty and Fiddle had run outside as soon as they heard the wagon, and the first thing Desty missed was Papa's loud "Halloo" which he always called when he saw them coming.

Instead of handing Burt the reins to lead Duke to the barn, Papa hobbled the horse outside a little distance from the barn and house. That was strange, very strange.

They followed Papa into the soddy and heard him tell Mama, "Bingle's daughter's horse died last night, from some kind of disease. I never thought of anything like that. We even hitched up Duke to the carcass to pull it off into the prairie."

There was a tired sound in his voice as he hung up his coat on a peg driven into the sod wall. "Of course, Bingle's son-in-law couldn't do much hobbling about on crutches."

For a while Papa sat silent, thoughtful, saying nothing. But he drank the strong black coffee Mama poured for him.

When he spoke at last, it seemed as though he were talking to himself. "It's too bad Bingle didn't know about it. I sure hope Duke didn't catch the plagued thing. But I asked Doc Wilson about it before we left town. He said it was something called anth— anth—"

"Anthrax," Burt said the word simply.

"Yes," Papa continued, "anthrax. Doc said if we see any sign to just keep him warm and quiet and away from other stock. There isn't much that could be done for him, Doc said. If it is only a slight case he'd get over it, otherwise he'd die."

"Try not to worry," Mama told him as she set out some fried salt pork and sliced some bread for him and Burt.

"I hope there's no need to worry," Papa answered. "But I'll have to watch Duke closely tonight."

Poor Papa. Desty thought of yesterday. It had been such a wonderful day. And now, such a short time later, everything was going wrong. What if they lost Duke too! Would that be the last straw, and would Mama and Papa give up at last? She thought of Blue Wing. But that only made her more mixed up. And she couldn't tell whether or not she would want to leave the Cherokee Strip now.

Fiddle, who was silent longer than she usually was, slid along the bench to Papa's end of the table. "Will Duke die?" she asked.

Papa jerked his head up. "I hope not, I hope not."

Desty wished desperately that she could help. "Couldn't we give Duke some kind of medicine?"

"Not that I know of," Papa pushed his plate away and stood up. "If he's caught it, he won't last long. It works fast."

Jason had stayed outside with Duke. Now he rushed in out of breath, the lantern which he had lit, still in his hand. "Papa, Duke looks awfully tired. Seems like he wants to lie down."

Papa ran through the door. Everyone followed. Taking the lantern Papa held it high to look at Duke, and shook his head sadly.

"He's got it, I know he's got it." He patted Duke's mane. "Get him some water."

But Duke did not seem to want the water. He moved slowly, bending his front knees as if he wanted to lie down, and then didn't want to. He breathed in short gasps, too.

Then for the first time, Desty remembered that Duke belonged to Uncle Luke.

Papa must have been thinking of the same thing. "I almost wish it were Champ instead. I hate to have to tell Luke we let his horse die."

Jason stepped up. "He's not dead yet. There must be some way to save him."

Just as he said that, Duke let his four legs buckle and lay down.

"I'm afraid not," Papa said, "but maybe if he could live through the night he might make it." He knelt beside the sick horse. "He's already having a hard time breathing. His throat is swelling." Duke neighed weakly and tried to raise his head. "He's having pain too."

Desty watched the beautiful, sleek head move, and each time it rose slightly only to fall back again.

All this time Burt had said nothing. Desty could not tell whether Duke's illness bothered him or not. She could not guess now if he was concerned, even when he spoke.

"It's too chilly out here for him. We'll have to rig up something to keep the cold off him." He peered through the semi-darkness as though looking for something to carry out his idea.

"You're right," Papa agreed.

They couldn't put Duke into the barn with Champ, or even near the fodder Champ would eat later. Not even near the stall or manger in case whatever Duke had was terribly catching as Doc Wilson said.

Burt drove four poles into the ground and stretched the canvas top of the wagon over them to make a three-sided shelter. Then he brought the horse blankets from the barn. After they covered Duke, Jason started a fire to keep him warm.

After that, Papa said he would sit out with him for a while and then the boys could take turns.

Desty could still picture Duke at the starting line when the signal sounded. How he threw his head up and his mane flew in the wind. He had looked as if he wanted the whole world to know that he was going to help Papa find a fine claim. Now look at him, lying there on the ground. She turned and went into the soddy with Mama and Fiddle. She felt she would cry if she stayed near Duke any longer.

Night settled down. Mama sent her and Fiddle to bed.

"But we could help watch Duke," Fiddle protested.

Mama shook her head. "Papa and the boys will do that. They know more about such things than you do."

But all night Desty could hear Papa and Burt and Jason changing about and taking turns with Duke. Now, if Duke would die, would Mama ask Papa to go back to Kansas? It always ended up the same way. To go back to their old home meant something awfully bad had to happen. She certainly did not want Duke to die in order to leave the Strip. She thought again of Blue Wing. What if the little Indian girl never wanted to become a friend? It was terrible to be so mixed up.

Each time she woke and heard Papa and the boys talk, they sounded more worried. Just before sunrise, she heard the door pushed open, and slow, dragging steps cross the floor.

It was Burt. "Duke's dead." There was a catch in his loud whisper to Mama and Papa. And Desty realized that Duke's dying *did* matter to Burt. He must have felt awfully hurt to sound like that.

She turned over, face down in her pillow. What would Papa do now? If he had to pay Uncle Luke back for Duke, would he give him Champ? If he did, what would they do? Surely then they would all go back to Kansas. But she was tired now, after all the times she woke during the night. And she did not want to think anymore. She slept.

Later, when she got up, Papa and the boys already had dug a ditch out on the prairie and buried Duke. They sat around the breakfast table planning their day. Mama was a little silent, but she went about her regular tasks.

Desty knew they were not leaving the Cherokee Strip yet.

Later in the day, after she had finished her chores, she crept into the bedroom, opened her treasure box and fingered the little bag of Kansas earth. Oh, why didn't they go back! The last two months had been so long. Autumn was slipping away. The cottonwoods along the creek had lost their leaves. So had the bushes on the bank. And all the grass was brown and dry. Their first Oklahoma winter would soon be with them.

It was a gray day and there was no sunset. Darkness came early and Desty wondered what she could do to make the evening less sad than the day was. She thought of Marietta, and, of course, missed her. Yesterday she had felt that Blue Wing's friendship would fill Marietta's place. Now she was not sure.

But for a long time, she had been meaning to write to Marietta. This evening would be a good time to do just that. Asking Mama for pen and paper, she and Fiddle very carefully worded a letter. Desty winced when she wrote of Duke's death.

Mama also wrote a letter, to Aunt Bessie and Uncle Luke, about Duke dying, and promising to make full payment for him.

Papa said nothing while Mama wrote. He sat on her rocker, slowly puffing on his pipe, and looking very discouraged.

Finally when Mama finished, folded and sealed the letter, he spoke.

"Well, Nell, I'm glad you do not want to give up, but I'm mighty sorry things turned out like this."

"We'll be all right, Henry," Mama said softly.

Papa took a deep pull on his pipe and said to everyone in general, "You know, Mama is quite a lady. She could have told us all to pack up and go back to Kansas any time, but she stuck with it like a champion partner."

Mama's cheeks grew pink. "Now, Henry, I only did what any other wife would do under the circumstances."

Papa held up his hand. "I speak the truth, Nell. It takes courage to go on when you don't want to and to do your best to make a good job of it."

Then he looked across the room, towards Desty. "I think Desty knows what I mean."

For a moment, Desty felt guilty. She had begun to think Papa didn't care how hard a time Mama had trying to make a new home for them, or about how the rest of the family felt living in the Strip.

But Papa had known and cared all the time. Desty felt proud. Never in her life again would she feel as proud as she did at that moment.

# Chapter
# Sixteen
## "It's our birthday"

They all breathed easier when they were certain that Champ showed no signs of having the anthrax that killed Duke. Still it was sad to see Papa burn the blankets and canvas and poles and everything else that had been near Duke.

But not until Uncle Luke answered Mama's letter, telling them not to worry, did Papa seem like himself again. Uncle Luke said he understood and that they did not have to settle up until they were better able to.

November ended with damp and chilly days. Papa seldom went to town now. There was no work. Their supplies dwindled away. Mama cooked one chicken after the other until there were only two left.

"I will need them to hatch some eggs in the Spring," she said.

They had plenty of turnips, though, and some cornmeal, molasses and a little flour left. That was all. Desty wondered how a family could get so poor so soon.

But Mama smiled knowingly and a little sadly. "It takes a lot to feed six mouths. But we're luckier than some others. We still have our cow."

December brought little change. Desty and Fiddle did not play outdoors as much as they used to. Mama feared they would catch cold.

The day before Christmas dawned gray and gloomy. The stove did not seem to get ahead of the dampness at all in the soddy. Papa said he was going to see Mr. Bingle.

"Maybe I could do a day's work in the store for a few groceries," he said. They had nothing left now except the turnips and a little cornmeal. "Lots of other men have gone all the way back to Kansas to find work." He scratched his head and smoothed back his bushy black hair. "Maybe I should do that, too. At least I might earn a few dollars that way."

"No," Mama said, and her soft gentle mouth was set in stern lines. "We've stuck together so far. We'll go right on sticking. If things get that bad, we'll all move back together."

Desty felt her heart jump within her. She looked at Papa quickly, but he only agreed with Mama. "Yes, you're right. We'll make it in the Strip itself, or not at all."

Then he left for town by himself. "If I get some work with Bingle, I'll have to stay at the store all day," he explained.

When suppertime came and he did not return, Mama said they would not wait for him. "If there was no work at the store, Papa may have looked for other odd jobs. No telling how far he went or when he'll be through." But Mama's eyes were worried. Desty knew she wondered if Papa were really working or if something had happened to him.

Everyone was silent as Mama dished out the boiled turnips. Desty thought she would choke if she had to eat another turnip. But she was hungry and managed to force down a little. She guessed she should not feel that way about turnips. After all, if it weren't for turnips, the Shawns would be half-starved, but that did not make her like them.

She looked around from Mama to Burt, to Jason and Fiddle. Everyone was settling down to a dragging, damp, discouraging evening, like so many others lately. Perhaps if Papa were home he would start singing or telling stories or something.

Mama began her endless mending. She always said she had to keep their clothes in as good a condition as possible. Desty knew that was because they could not tell when they would be able to get new ones. But tonight Mama stuck her needle in and out much more quickly than other times. And she was silent, not clucking her tongue over the tear in Burt's pants, or laughing at the big hole in the toe of Jason's stocking. She just kept looking down at her task and stabbing the needle in and out.

Tomorrow was Christmas Day!

Desty thought of how it would be if they still lived back in Kansas. They would probably be hanging up stockings, trimming a tree, nibbling Christmas cookies and singing carols. Mama would be checking to see if she had everything for their turkey dinner: celery for the bread stuffing; cranberries, sweet potatoes, and chili sauce; tomatoes and jelly she had put up the summer before; and of course, big pumpkin pies.

And they would all lay out their clothes for church. Later, Desty and Fiddle would sneak up to their bedroom to wrap their presents for the others and the boys would try to guess what they were. Papa would be sitting in his arm chair smoking his pipe, and telling Mama how good everything smelled. Then when they were all settled, he would roast chestnuts for them.

She should not be thinking of those things, Desty told herself, but she only felt worse. She almost had to cry now when she looked around the crowded, chilly soddy. Heaven only knew how much longer it would have to be their home.

The rough benches and bedsteads Papa had made hurriedly when they first came here fitted right in with the earth wall and board floor. The rough table did too, and the three shelves along the wall. But the coal oil lamp with its base of painted pink roses looked as out of place as a huge jewel would be setting in a mud puddle.

Burt sat in the corner in silence on a three-legged stool, leaning his back against the sod walls. Desty could never bring herself to lean against the walls, for fear that maybe some bugs or worms would still be hiding in the earth among the grass roots, even though Mama had covered the lower half of the wall with cloth. Desty knew Fiddle didn't care. If Fiddle found a bug she would just double up her fist and smash it. Desty shivered at the thought.

Burt just sat there staring straight ahead. Desty wondered what he was thinking. He had gone back to being awfully quiet, the way he had been before they moved down here. His grownup actions and talk after he helped Papa stake the claim and start homesteading seemed to be gone. Now he was always scowling, and not saying much.

Desty caught Mama looking at him several times today.

Desty guessed the reason he was sullen was that Papa had gone to town without him. He almost always accompanied Papa, and the day was long just sitting in the soddy without much to do besides his chores.

Jason was fidgeting and walking around the small space restlessly, but finally he settled himself on the end of the bench where she and Fiddle sat. They had been leafing through the old dog-eared magazines.

Jason looked at one and threw it aside. "Gee, Christmas will seem funny, with no tree or anything," he said.

Mama quickly sucked her thumb where she must have stuck it with the needle.

"Well, we're all together. And Christmas is Christmas even without a tree," she told Jason. "Besides, there's the real meaning of the first Christmas, remember."

"I know, I know, but —" Jason looked towards Burt. "Do you think we could —"

"No," Burt snapped. "I don't want to do anything."

Desty wondered what Jason wanted to do, probably play a game. She was tempted to tell him about the presents she and Fiddle had hidden away. That might make him feel better, but it would spoil the surprise, and she knew Fiddle would not like that. They had hemmed white handkerchiefs from pieces of an old sheet Mama had given them, for Papa, Burt and Jason. And they had made a little pin cushion, stuffed with dry grass, for Mama.

Soon Fiddle grew restless, too. She went to the top shelf along the wall and got Papa's shoe blackening. Then she took off her shoes and placed them on a piece of old paper on top of the table. They were her everyday shoes, but they were stretched out and more comfortable than her better ones. First she smeared a band of polish around the middle of one shoe, held it up to look at it, then began to polish the rest of it.

Jason took one glance at it and started to laugh. He laughed out loud and kept it up.

"What's so funny?" Burt asked.

"Look, polishing her shoes! What for? Are we going to a fancy Christmas party? Look at the difference! One all muddy —"

Fiddle began to cry. She must have felt awfully hurt, or she would have snapped back at Jason. Instead, she sat there crying.

"It's our birthday," she sobbed.

Desty did not know what to say. She hadn't mentioned their birthday all day because she did not want to hurt Mama. She was surprised that Fiddle waited this long to speak of it.

Desty glanced quickly at Mama. For a moment Mama looked as though she might cry, too. Then she put down her sewing and patted Fiddle's shoulder. "Sh-h, it's all right. I was waiting for Papa so we could all sing "Happy Birthday" together. But everything will be all —"

Suddenly Burt jumped up from his stool and hit Jason alongside the head so hard he toppled off the end of the bench. "Keep your silly mouth shut if you have to make everybody feel bad."

Desty did not have to guess what Burt was thinking at that moment, and she liked him a lot more than she ever did before. But then again, she didn't think he should have hit Jason.

Jason got to his feet and lunged towards Burt, but Mama stepped forward. Jason was pointing his finger. "You hit me again and I'll knock your block off."

Burt turned his back on him. "Well, call out the militia beforehand." He sat down on the stool in the corner again.

Desty thought of Kansas. She never remembered the boys as anything but pals back there. Now they seemed to look at everything differently. What kind of place was the Cherokee Strip if it made brothers disagree and fight?

Mama pushed Jason back towards the bench. "Behave yourselves, right now, both of you."

Surely Mama would see how badly things were going now, Desty thought. She looked at Mama and said cautiously, "Maybe we should all go back to Kansas."

"No," Mama answered. "Not yet. You have to give a new thing every chance before you turn away from it." Then she patted Fiddle's shoulder again and went back to her sewing.

Fiddle wiped her eyes and continued polishing her shoes.

But when Jason looked at the shoes setting there, one all muddy and one half-polished, they must have struck him funny all over again. He pointed to them and put his hand over his mouth, and even though he made no sound, his shoulders shook and his eyes were bright with laughter.

Fiddle watched him for a minute, her face sober. Then she looked at the shoes and giggled. The two of them sat there shaking in silent laughter until Desty had to grin. Then Mama did. Before they finished Burt joined in.

"What a silly family," he said. He glanced at Jason. "Sorry I hit you." Then as quickly as he started, he stopped laughing and leaned back against the wall, silent once more.

A moment later the door was pushed open and Papa came in. "I thought I heard a lot of noise in here a minute ago. What's going on?"

"Just my shoes," Fiddle said, holding them up. "Everybody thinks they're funny."

Fiddle had said the right thing at the right time. Again Desty was surprised at her.

Everyone gathered around as Papa placed a bag on the table. "Merry Christmas!" he said. "I worked all day at Bingle's." He opened the bag and spread out some groceries that were badly needed — sugar, flour, salt-pork, molasses, salt and a little sack of coffee. Last he opened a carefully wrapped package and showed them a small square fruit cake and a half dozen candy sticks.

"My day's wages didn't stretch far enough for a turkey, but we'll manage," Papa said, grinning. Then he pointed to the fruit cake. "And that is a birthday cake, for guess who?"

Papa hadn't forgotten either. Desty just looked at him. "Oh, thank you, Papa."

Fiddle joined in. "Thank you, Papa." Then she lifted the cake close to her face. "It smells so good."

Mama's face was all happiness as she stood there clasping and unclasping her hands. "I thought you had no luck at the store and went on looking," she told Papa. "But this — this is all so wonderful. We needed these things so badly."

"Something else is wonderful," Papa told them, glancing excited from one to the other. "I am going to work next week for Bingle. He's not feeling well and the store is in a mess. He said he'd like to sell the business if he could get it going good enough to pay off his debts first." Papa turned to Mama and grasped her forearms. "Wouldn't it be great if we could buy the store, Nell? We'd have money coming in to build the new house, to buy seed and another horse."

Burt's face looked like one great big smile, it was so bright. Desty knew he liked the idea of a store. Papa always said Burt had a good head for business.

## Chapter Seventeen
# A Visitor for Christmas

E ven though it had been dark for some time, Christmas Eve was young yet. Burt stabled Champ while Papa sat down to the warmed-over turnips. Mama put some coffee on to boil and set right to work kneading some dough for white bread. She would set it to rise overnight by the chimney.

"Oh, please, can't we have some candy?" Fiddle pleaded as she and Desty put the groceries away for Mama.

"Well, a little," Mama said as she scraped the dough from her fingers and reached for the bag. "We want to save some for tomorrow." She broke two sticks in half, and gave the boys and Desty and Fiddle each a piece.

How foolish the boys were to chew theirs up right away, Desty thought. She and Fiddle sucked theirs for a long time. Desty still wished they had a Christmas tree, but she hoped no one would mention it. She did not want anyone to feel unhappy again.

Suddenly the lamp began to flicker and grow dim. "My goodness," Mama said, "I thought there was more oil in the lamp than that." She wiped her hands on her apron and shook the coal oil can that stood by the door. "Empty as can be. Well, we'll just have to use some candles!"

Papa shook his head while he lighted two candles, one for the table, and one for the highest shelf.

"I clean forgot about oil," he said. "Or I would have brought some."

But the candles threw a nice soft light around the soddy, giving a cozy look to everything.

Mama was all finished with the bread dough now, and she drew Desty and Fiddle close to her. "I think it is time to sing "Happy Birthday" to the girls."

They were singing at the top of their voices, when a knock at the door startled them. Who could possibly be calling on Christmas Eve? That was a night everyone stayed home.

As Papa opened the door, the candles' light fell on a short plump woman in a fringed jacket, headscarf and mittens.

"Granny Buckskin!" Fiddle cried and darted around the table.

Granny's round face broke into a wide grin and its fullness spread up into folds around her eyes, making them like two shiny black shoebuttons. Papa caught Fiddle's arm and drew her aside.

"Come in, come in," he said opening the door as wide as possible.

But when Granny stepped in they could see she was not alone. A thin little halfbreed girl with large dark eyes moved quietly into the soddy with her.

"Oh, Blue Wing! Mama, this is Blue Wing." Desty could not keep her excitement from showing. But she did not want to either. This was such a wonderful surprise.

Granny set two heavy cloth bags on the table and then stood behind Blue Wing with her hands on the girl's narrow shoulders. "Blue Wing, this is Mrs. Shawn and her boys Burt and Jason. You met the girls and Mr. Shawn in town." Granny's rich voice was as clear and bell-like as ever.

Blue Wing nodded and looked timidly from one to the other. She did not speak. Oh, dear, Desty thought, what if she won't talk to us at all.

Mama cleared off a stool. "We're glad to have you, Blue Wing. Won't you sit down?" Papa gave the rocking chair to Granny.

Mama asked, "Did you have supper yet?"

"Oh my yes," Granny answered. "We had an early supper."

"Well, you must at least have a cup of coffee," Mama went on, "and I'm sure Blue Wing likes milk."

"Thank you, that will be fine," Granny nodded to Blue Wing to accept the milk. "But I can't stay too long. I don't like to ride alone in the wagon across the prairie in the late hours."

What could she mean, ride alone across the prairie?

Maybe Papa did not know either, but he said he would be glad to accompany her back to town.

Then Granny explained that her daughter in Wichita was ill and that she would like to take the morning train to visit her over the holiday.

"But I'm really here on account of Blue Wing," Granny continued. "Her mother has to work right through the holidays. As I told Mr. Shawn in town, she is not allowed to keep Blue Wing with her. That is why Blue Wing stays with me while she works."

Desty wondered why some white people did not want their children to associate with Indian boys and girls. It seemed cruel. But the Abernathys paid well, and Blue Wing's mother kept the job so that she could provide a home for them, even though it was just a little hut on the prairie. It seemed a shame they could spend so little time together in it.

Granny was looking for a place for Blue Wing to stay until after New Year's when she herself would be returning to Barryville. Desty almost asked why Blue Wing could not go with Granny to Wichita, but she thought that question would be impolite. It would sound as though she did not want Blue Wing to stay with them. And she did, she did!

Granny, however, explained. "Blue Wing's mother likes to see her every day, so she comes to my place for a little visit when she gets a chance. If I took Blue Wing with me, it would be over a week until she could see her again. Neither one of them likes the idea of Blue Wing going such a distance away."

At the mention of Wichita, Blue Wing's eyes widened a little and she seemed anxious. Granny patted her shoulder and then turned to Mama.

"I wouldn't be bothering you so late, but I tried several families. They couldn't keep her for one reason or another. I told her mother I would find a place for her and that she could visit her at the laundry tomorrow the same as any other day." Granny looked at Papa. "About the middle of the afternoon, if that wouldn't be too much trouble."

Papa assured her it would be no trouble at all.

Granny continued, "And if you'll take her to their little house on the prairie for the weekends, that's all they'll expect."

Again, Papa assured her he would, and Mama added, "We'll be glad to have her."

Desty was so happy she could have jumped for joy. But when she looked at Blue Wing's blank little face, she felt deep sympathy for her. Blue Wing probably had been afraid that the Shawn family would not want her either. That must be a terrible feeling, to have people avoid you or not want you.

Fiddle as usual, found her tongue quicker than Desty or the boys. "A visitor for Christmas is like a present for the whole family."

Once more this evening, Fiddle had said the right thing, the most right thing she ever could have said.

At the word "present", Granny took her cloth bags from the table. "Speaking of gifts, this is a lean Christmas for everyone. But I have something I want to give you. They're secondhand, but you can still enjoy them." Out of the bag she took three books, four magazines and four newspapers. Desty thought she would burst with excitement.

"I have finished with them," Granny said. "The books were my daughter's long ago. I'm sure the girls will like them."

Never, never were there nicer presents — a new friend, books to read, magazines to look at. Desty could hardly wait for tomorrow.

Then Granny handed Mama a package. "A little treat for your Christmas dinner. But don't open it until tomorrow."

"Why not stay the night here?" Papa asked. "With an early start, you could get to the depot in time for the train."

"Yes, please do," Mama pleaded. Her eyes were sparkling. Desty was certain that Mama was thinking how delightful it would be to have a good "woman" chat with Granny.

But Granny said no. "I would love to but it was a busy day at the laundry, and I have some personal things to attend to and some packing to do. The train leaves early, so I'll have to have everything ready."

Then as Mama poured her another cup of coffee, Granny looked around. "No Christmas tree?"

"No, we don't have any pines on our land and we weren't able to buy one in town," Mama told her.

"Well, maybe I could help you make one."

Jason jumped up. "Make one?" The way he asked showed that he had been wishing for a tree too.

"Yes," Granny answered. She turned to Mama. "Do you have any cotton batting?"

"Just some I've been saving for a quilt." Mama answered. "But I suppose we could use some of it."

"If you boys get me a little sapling with a few branches,

we could make a very pretty tree." Granny told them.

Burt and Jason grabbed their jackets and were out of the door in a flash. And they came back quickly too, their cheeks and noses red with the cold, carrying a small tree. They were real pals again, Desty noticed.

Granny stood the tree in a bucket and forced a few pieces of firewood around its slim trunk to make it stand upright. Then she took the cotton batting and carefully wrapped it around every branch and twig.

"Just take it off carefully afterwards, and you can still use it for your quilt," she explained.

When she finished, the tree was beautiful, just as it would have been after a heavy snowfall.

Desty was beginning to wonder what they would use for trimmings now that they had a tree, when Mama surprised them still further. She took a little box of ornaments out of the trunk. "I just brought a few along with us, but they are the prettiest we had."

Never was there a lovelier tree. Though Blue Wing did not say a word, her eyes showed her delight.

"Well," Granny said at last, "I hate to go but I must."

Papa brought her horse and wagon to the door, and then went back to the barn for Champ. He would ride in Granny's wagon with her to town and then ride Champ home. Granny left amid a shower of Merry Christmas greetings.

It was close to midnight when Papa returned. Desty and Fiddle and Blue Wing and the boys had been in bed for hours. All of them seemed to be asleep, except Desty. She could not sleep, she was far too excited.

After Papa came home, Desty could hear him and Mama talking and laughing softly. She could also hear a

soft rustle that told her they were leafing through the magazines and newspapers. Then she knew she was not the only one who missed reading matter, even though Papa brought back the word-of-mouth news every time he went to town.

Snuggling down beneath the covers, Desty wondered how she could have wanted to leave the Strip so short a time ago. She guessed it was because she was afraid Blue Wing would always be stand-offish and hard to speak to. She knew better now; Blue Wing would be her friend.

# Chapter
## Eighteen
# "It was good
# to see my mother"

Christmas Day dawned clear and frosty. Desty's waking thought was of the first Christmas morning so long ago, and she twisted her head around to look up at the picture over her bed. Her next thought was that now she and Fiddle were eleven years old. It did not seem much different from being ten years old, though. Last year Marietta had come to supper on their birthday.

Desty looked down at Blue Wing still sound asleep beside Fiddle. How different Blue Wing was from Marietta. Yet she felt she wanted to be as close to her as she was to Marietta.

Mama was cooking breakfast and humming a carol.

It was good to hear Mama humming to herself again. She had not done so lately.

Just as Desty peeked out at her, Mama gave the kettle a last stir and tapped the wooden spoon on its edge.

Then Mama called," "Merry Christmas, everyone!"

And instantly they all were awake, calling from their beds, "Merry Christmas, Merry Christmas!"

Blue Wing blinked in surprise at the gay shouts. Then Desty remembered that it was not a holiday that Indians celebrated. But she took Blue Wing's hand and said Merry Christmas, anyway. Much to her surprise and joy, Blue Wing smiled, and her thin, dark face lit up so rapidly, Desty hugged her.

Fiddle scurried past them, calling, "We forgot to put the presents under the tree."

So they did! Last evening had been so exciting, they forgot. But there was no present for Blue Wing! Desty went quickly to her treasure box and took out one of her shiny, smooth stones. Then under the tree they found other presents, from Mama. Mufflers! The color of the wool was familiar. Why, it was from the old sweater of Papa's that Mama hid so quickly when they came home from town that day last month. Desty guessed Mama got enough wool for the other mufflers from other cast-off sweaters which she unraveled.

Everyone exclaimed over the gifts Desty and Fiddle made. Even when Mama said, "Sit down to breakfast now before everything is cold," she held the pin-cushion they gave her.

Desty never enjoyed a breakfast any more than she enjoyed this one. There beside her sat her new friend, and over in the corner stood the most beautiful white tree that she had ever seen. And beneath it lay the magazines and books Granny had brought.

Blue Wing ate slowly with one hand, while she held her long braids out of the way with the other. She did not look up from her bowl at all. Desty wished she were not so shy. Maybe when she and Fiddle had her to themselves she would not be so bashful. After all, being in the middle of a whole family of strangers would make anyone shy.

While they were helping Mama with the beds, the dishes, and straightening up, Desty suddenly remembered something.

"Mama, why don't you fix our hair in curls like you always used to for Christmas?"

Mama's face brightened. She fingered Desty's coppery hair. "Why, yes, I think I shall. But we'll have to hurry. Before long it will be time to start dinner."

Fiddle pouted, though. She did not want to leave the drawing she was making of some reindeer for Blue Wing. "Oh, fiddle-dee-dee! Our braids are good enough. Besides, Blue Wing has braids."

"Oh, but Mama can fix hers too." Desty said. It would be wonderful to see Blue Wing's lovely, black hair in curls.

Fiddle still pouted. "Well, I'm going to keep right on drawing, while Mama is fixing mine."

Mama just sat behind each one with her strips of cloth and wound their curls up tight. Blue Wing must have liked the idea because she undid her braids in a hurry. As her black hair fell free on her shoulders, she smiled. Then after Mama had dampened it and combed it and tied it in curls, Blue Wing's neck seemed much longer and more slender and her dark eyes flashed in satisfaction.

When Jason surveyed the three girls all with multi-colored strips of cloth woven through their hair, he called them rag heads. They only laughed.

There was still one more surprise for them — the package Granny left. Before Mama started preparing dinner, she opened it, and found some delicious dried fruit — prunes, apricots and raisins.

What a lovely treat. Mama stewed some of the dried fruit for dinner, and since they had to be careful of the supplies, they had turnips again. But there would be some saltpork with them and white bread. It seemed a strange Christmas dinner, but even turnips tasted better today.

After they finished, no one seemed anxious to leave the table. Everyone talked and laughed so much they even had Blue Wing joining in. Then Jason suggested singing "Adeste Fidelis," not only for Christmas, but for Desty's and Fiddle's birthday.

Desty explained to Blue Wing how they got their names.

Blue Wing was fascinated and volunteered to tell them about her own name. "My mother said, when I was born my father said I was as pretty as the wing of a bluebird." She lowered her eyes and grew shy again.

Then Jason burst forth with "Deck the Halls with Boughs of Holly" and again everyone joined in.

Mama waited until the last verse and stood up. "You all go right on singing, but I want to start cleaning up."

It was nice of Mama not to ask their help, Desty thought, but she got up from the table anyway and so did Fiddle and Blue Wing. Before long they had the dishes washed, dried and stacked. They shook out the table cloth and swept the floor. And all the while Papa and the boys kept them entertained with every Christmas song they could think of.

Finally Papa held up his hand to halt the singing. "If Blue Wing wants to see her mother, I better be driving her into town. And I think Desty and Fiddle should go along to keep her company."

That was exactly what Desty wished. First they took the curler strips out of Blue Wing's hair and their own. Blue Wing's hair was a beautiful surprise. It hung loose and curly at the ends and gave her pointed, narrow face a wonderful prettiness. Mama rummaged in her work-basket for a ribbon, and found a bright red one. Bunching several curls together on the right side, she tied them tight in a lovely bow.

Desty could not get over how pretty Blue Wing looked. "You're just like a picture." Blue Wing's light copper face turned a little rosier.

"You sure are," Fiddle assured her. Desty could see Mama was pleased that Blue Wing's hair turned out so nice.

Then they put on extra pairs of warm stockings, and their coats and scarves, and the mufflers Mama made for them. Mama also hurriedly looked for an extra scarf for Blue Wing and told her to keep warm.

The wagon tracks on the prairie were frozen into uneven ruts and the edges of the ruts were worn smooth by the strong winds forever blowing across them. The wind stung their noses and cheeks and they had to talk loudly to be heard before the wind swept their words away.

Papa clucked his tongue at Champ and let the reins

slap down gently on the horse's blanketed back. Champ quickened his gait and the seven miles to town were soon covered. Before Desty realized it, they were turning down the main street.

All the pine wood buildings were already weather-stained. This time last year, Desty thought, this was all wild and free. Here and there she could see a face at a window. Sometimes a door opened and someone called, "Hello Hank, hello girls. Merry Christmas!"

When someone asked them to come in for a visit, Papa always said, "Thanks anyway, but we can't right now."

On they went, clippety-clop, clippety-clop down to Granny's laundry shop. Papa fitted the key in the lock and opened the door. The smell of soap and stale wash water met them as they stepped inside.

They all warmed up quickly after getting out of the cold wind, and soon Papa said, "It's almost three o'clock. You better meet your mother, Blue Wing, and bring her here."

Blue Wing went out without a word and turned north. Her mother would be waiting under the huge bare oak tree at the end of the street.

As Blue Wing's lonely figure moved up the street, Desty felt a great pity for her. The only family Blue Wing had was her mother, and she had to meet her like a fugitive. If her mother came to the laundry ahead of them, there might be someone who might see her and accuse her of trying to break in. There were many in town who did not look favorably at Indians.

How could Mrs. Abernathy, or anyone else, be so cruel as to expect a woman to work and not see her child on Christmas Day? Oh, Desty knew Indians did not care

much about Christmas. She knew, too, that Mrs. Abernathy did not mind Blue Wing's mother seeing her, as
long as it was far enough away from the big Abernathy
home. It might be wrong to hate someone, but if it were
not wrong, Desty told herself, she would hate Mrs. Abernathy right now.

Desty wondered too, how an Indian woman could
work for white people who treated her so indifferently,
even for good pay. But Blue Wing had told them her
mother talked of sending her through school to the higher
grades, maybe even to college.

Desty tried to picture how it felt to be a halfbreed. Did
Blue Wing ever want to be all Indian or all white?

Her thoughts were cut short when Papa said, "Here
they come."

When she saw them Desty was surprised. She had expected Blue Wing's mother to be much older, short and
stocky like so many of the Indian women she had seen
traveling through Kansas. Instead she was a straight,
slender young woman, with shiny, black braids resting
on her collar-bones. Her face was lean and expressionless, and she clutched a faded, folded blanket about the
shoulders of her dark cotton dress. Her feet were covered
with mocassins.

As they came through the doorway, she gave them the
briefest nod, and went on into the living quarters to
which Papa pointed and said, "You and Blue Wing can
visit in there."

When the flimsy door closed behind them, Fiddle
opened her mouth to say something, but Papa put his
fingers on his lips to quiet her. Desty could not blame

Fiddle for wanting to ask questions, but she knew this was not the time to be curious about their new friend's mother.

No sound came from behind the door and the visit was a very short one. When Blue Wing and her mother stepped back into the washing room, Papa and the girls stared at them, and Fiddle's gasp could easily be heard. Blue Wing's hair was pulled severely back and braided tightly again into her two side braids. The red ribbon was gone. She looked down at the floor and said nothing.

But her mother looked at them, sharply. Her face was still expressionless and stony, but her black eyes glinted as she glanced from one to the other.

Desty felt she must be disliking them all very much at that moment. Though silent, she seemed to be saying, "My daughter does not have to copy a white girl's hair style to be as good as one."

At the door, she turned to Papa and said in very good English but in a flat, even tone, "Thank you for bringing her." Then she stepped through the doorway and was gone. Blue Wing stood there looking awfully lonely.

"What happened to —" Fiddle began and Desty gave her a jab in the ribs with her elbow. She knew Fiddle was going to be nosy about Blue Wing's hair.

Desty hoped with all her might that Blue Wing's mother would not think badly of them and forbid Blue Wing to be their friend.

But as they were heading home in the wagon, Blue Wing smiled and said, "It was good to see my mother." She touched her braids but offered no explanation. Blue Wing looked all Indian again, but that did not matter —

Blue Wing was the same Blue Wing and Desty liked her very much.

The afternoon had gone quickly. A light snowfall had started, swirling down like tiny, white feathers through the dusk that settled about them before they reached home. The wind kept blowing across the fields, whistling and sifting the snowflakes in between the long brown blades of grass.

Above them, dark wintry clouds scudded across the sky as though they were trying to outrun the wind. Somehow the Strip looked different to Desty today. The bleakness was still there on the landscape but inside herself it was wearing away. Today she felt more certain that she could learn to really like this place after all.

The warmth of the soddy felt good after the long ride, and the smell of Mama's supper made them get off their coats in a hurry. Desty went straight to the table and set the places. She could see Mama and the boys looking at Blue Wing's braids, and was glad they said nothing.

The evening was a quiet, happy one. It wore away with games, singing Christmas songs, and looking at the books and magazines.

Just before they stepped into the bedroom to get ready for bed, Blue Wing went to Mama and handed her the folded up red ribbon. "My mother likes my hair this way." She touched her braids again.

Mama smiled and pressed the ribbon back into Blue Wing's hand. "Your hair would look lovely in any style. And you may keep the ribbon."

Then Blue Wing's face was brightened by her wonderful smile.

# Chapter
## Nineteen
# Back to Kansas?

January 4th arrived and still Granny had not returned. Desty and Fiddle enjoyed having Blue Wing. Desty even secretly wished that Granny would stay much longer in Wichita. But Blue Wing's eyes were growing more anxious each day. Desty guessed that she feared Granny might not come back at all. And if Granny did not come back for her, where would she live from now on?

One day Fiddle asked bluntly, "Would you like to live with us always?"

For a moment Blue Wing's face brightened, then straightened quickly. "Yes, but this is your family. You belong to each other. I don't."

"You would if you would stay," Desty assured her at once.

"No," Blue Wing's face now was as blank as it was the first time they saw her. "I live with Granny Buckskin. And when my mother is not working, I live with my mother."

Again Fiddle was blunt. "If your mother didn't work in town, would you live on the Reservation?"

"Yes, with my people."

Oh, what if something happened and Blue Wing *did* go back to the Reservation? Desty could not bear the thought of losing her. Then she remembered Blue Wing wanting to go to school. Only lately Papa had mentioned that there was news that a school would be built soon.

"But if you want to go to our school, you'll have to live near it. Don't you want to go to our school?"

"If I'm allowed to," Blue Wing answered.

Now, who would not allow Blue Wing to attend school, Desty wondered. But anyway they still had her with them. Suddenly Desty hugged her.

"No matter who you live with, you will always be our best friend in the Strip."

The blank look vanished from Blue Wing's face, and a wonderful "thank you" look took its place.

That evening a rider, passing by, brought a note from Granny. She was back in Barryville and she would be out in the morning to see them and to take Blue Wing back with her. The news made Blue Wing very happy. Her eyes no longer held that worried look.

Granny arrived in the middle of the next morning, her arms loaded with bundles.

"I'm so sorry to have imposed on you so long, Nell," she told Mama in her rich, clear voice. "But my daughter was quite ill. She had a severe cold in her lungs."

"You did not impose at all," Mama assured her, helping with the bundles.

By the way Fiddle was fidgeting, Desty knew she was wondering the same thing: What was in the packages? She hoped Fiddle would not ask outright what was in them. Mama would be embarrassed by such bad manners.

But Granny did not keep them in suspense very long. "My daughter has a new sewing machine. It was her Christmas gift from her husband. The last two days I was there she was able to get out of bed, and I was helping her learn how to run it," she explained.

"I went to the dry goods store and bought some dress goods." Granny looked at Desty, Fiddle and Blue Wing. "So, our three little girls here shall each have a new Christmas dress, even if I am a little late with them."

The dresses were solid colors with wide sashes. Desty's and Fiddle's were green, and Blue Wing's was blue.

"Yours is just like your name," Fiddle said.

Blue Wing smiled one of her merriest smiles, her dark eyes flashing. "Oh, thank you," she said to Granny, and Desty could guess how much this woman in the buckskin jacket meant to her.

Desty and Fiddle, remembering their manners, chorused, "Thank you, thank you."

Mama seemed delightfully surprised by the gifts. "But Granny, how can we repay you for such kindness?"

"Pay me!" Granny sounded a little unbelieving. "Why, I've been overpaid already. It is I who must thank you for keeping Blue Wing for almost two weeks."

"She could stay forever, if she wants to," Fiddle declared.

Blue Wing edged over towards Granny. Granny put her arm around her thin shoulders. "Blue Wing is grateful, I'm sure, but she is nearer her mother by staying with me." Granny's voice was full of bells.

Again Blue Wing's smile flashed in thanks to Granny.

Mama lifted the steaming tea kettle from the stove, and stirred the soup that was still cooking. "Take off your things and have some lunch with us."

Granny sat down heavily after removing her jacket. Then she opened another package. Desty had already guessed what was in it. Homesteaders almost always brought little gifts of food when visiting. They did not want a housewife to be left short of supplies on account of making extra food ready for them.

Granny was always more than generous. She had brought some sugar, molasses, rice and cornmeal.

It was nearly one-thirty when Granny and Blue Wing climbed onto the wagon seat for the ride back to Barryville. Suddenly Desty remembered about the school to be built.

Before Granny could slap the reins down and call Giddap, Desty called to her. "Granny, Blue Wing can go to school when it is built, can't she?"

Granny looked surprised. "Well, I surely hope so. I can't see why not. I'm certain her mother would like her to."

Well, if it was all right with Blue Wing's mother and Granny, then who could keep Blue Wing from attending school? Desty guessed that she was just worrying for nothing. Blue Wing smiled and waved to them.

That evening when Papa came home from work at Bingle's store, he told them that a meeting had been scheduled to discuss the new school. He said classes would likely start in a month or so.

Mama smiled. "I'm so glad," she said, "that's one thing that bothered me — no school, even though we saw to it that the children did their lessons regularly."

"Well, I'd just as soon keep on doing lessons regularly," Jason scowled, "as go to some old school every day."

"Me too!" Fiddle said. "We live too far away anyway."

"No, you don't." Papa smiled. "And you'll all go except Burt. I don't want to raise a bunch of ignoramusessssss." He laughed, saying he didn't know how to end that word.

"Oh, fiddle-dee-dee!" Fiddle muttered. The next moment she caught Desty's arm. "Come on, let's put our new dresses on again to show Papa."

The following week the meeting was held in town and it was planned that a school would be built midway between their claim and Barryville. Another school was going to be built on the eastern edge of Barryville for the children on claims just east of it. Most of the town children would go to that one.

Papa said he would take them in the wagon on his way to work in the morning and they could walk home in the afternoon.

Again Jason scowled. "That's three and a half miles."

Papa laughed. "Good exercise, good exercise."

Several nice sunny days followed, one after the other. It was good to wake up to bright clear weather. The air was warmed by the sun, and Mama let them run outdoors as much as they pleased.

Papa began buying lumber again and gave the boys

instructions for doing some of the work on the new house. They started on the walls where they had left off.

"We have to get as much done as possible before school starts," Burt said, teasing Jason.

"You're so funny," Jason said, "you should give clown lessons."

But their good luck was short-lived. One day Papa came home looking very downhearted. "We'll have to stop building our house again," he told them. "I'm out of work. Bingle's son-in-law is going to work in the store." Papa spit the words out disgustedly. "Clumsy oaf! He can't handle a lamp chimney without breaking it."

Papa sank down on the bench at the table, without taking his coat off. "I guess that's the end of my buying the business." His voice was weary. He reached into his pocket. "Two letters at the post-office for us. One's from Bessie and Luke. Maybe we should write them that we're all moving back to Kansas. Might as well if we can't build a decent house or earn a little money."

Papa handed the other letter to Desty. It was from Marietta.

Desty just stood there with the letter in her hand. Go back to Kansas, Papa had said! How discouraged he must be. At one time she would have been wildly happy to hear those words. But not now.

Lately she had not even looked into her treasure box at the little bag of Kansas earth. And she had not wished for them to return to Kansas since Blue Wing stayed with them.

Secretly she was beginning to like the Cherokee Strip. She knew now that she wanted to stay there, to live there always.

Fiddle grabbed the letter out of her hand and was turning it around inspecting it, while Mama was reading Aunt Bessie's. Any other time two such letters would have made Desty very excited. Now she just waited to hear what they had written.

Mama did not read the whole letter, but she told them parts of it. "Aunt Bessie sends her love to everyone. So does Uncle Luke. She says they had a lovely Christmas, but that they missed us. She says that she will send the things Santa left under their tree for us."

Jason laughed. "Christmas is getting better and better. It's lasting much longer this year."

Jason's laugh broke up the tight feeling in the soddy, but Papa only smiled. He did not join Jason in laughing as he usually did.

Fiddle was jiggling Desty's arm. "Come on, let's read Marietta's letter."

Fiddle had already opened it and was bursting with eagerness. She did not seem to care what Papa had said about moving back to their old home.

"Oh, Fiddle-dee-dee!" she moaned. "Marietta's writing is hard to read. Here you read it."

Desty took the letter and read it slowly. Marietta's writing was firm but some of her abc's were not too plain. Then one line stood out very plainly, and Desty felt worse than ever. She read it aloud slowly.

"Marietta says, 'I have met a new girl friend who just moved next door to the store. She is a nice girl with black hair and brown eyes. Her name is Belinda. I like her very much. How are you and Fiddle and your mother and'—"

Desty stopped. She felt as though Marietta had shut a door in her face and turned a key in the lock. Someone else was taking her place in Marietta's life.

"That's nice," Fiddle was saying. "Now Marietta isn't

alone any more. She has a new friend and so do we —
Blue Wing. Read some more."

At Fiddle's words, Desty felt very guilty. How selfish
she was, feeling bad because Marietta had a new friend.
She should be glad for her. And Fiddle was right, they
had Blue Wing. At the thought of Blue Wing she felt a
thousand times better.

She read on. "And how are your father and brothers?
We were all sorry to hear about Duke. Bouncey is dead
too. He was kicked by a horse and died the day after
Thanksgiving.' "

How sad, how terribly sad. Bouncey was such a sweet
little dog. Marietta needed a friend more than ever now.
It *was* nice that she found a new one.

Papa was talking about Mr. Bingle again. "Yes, and
I thought he was going to sell the store to me. He has
been talking about it for some time. He doesn't want the
responsibility of a business any more. And I got that
place running as smooth as satin. All cleaned up, with
good displays and everything." Papa ran his hand through
his busy hair. "Now that clumsy oaf of a son-in-law decided he'd like to try."

Mama filled Papa's coffee cup. "Calling names won't
help," she said. "We'll be all right."

Again their partly-finished house stood there, a big
lonely, empty framework. And again the soddy seemed
more crowded than ever, because their hopes of soon
moving out of it were shattered.

A spell of bad weather, cold and bleak, with gray skies,
did not help matters.

Desty thought more and more about school. At least
the idea of going to school again was a cheerful one. If

only Mama and Papa would not decide to move back to Kansas.

January ended and the school was built. Classes were to begin in the middle of February. There was going to be an afternoon social the Saturday before school opened, to introduce the teacher and let the parents enroll their children.

The social was to be held in the dining hall of a newly-built hotel in town, directly across from the railway depot.

That was something to look forward to. She would see Blue Wing and Granny again. And after that she would see Blue Wing at school every day. Again the world looked bright to Desty and she tried not to worry about moving away from the Strip.

But she couldn't help thinking that Mama had never sent back to Aunt Bessie for her good linens and chinaware. She had never hung up her windchime. And Papa's house slippers were still new in their box in the bedroom.

## Chapter Twenty
# The School Social

On the morning of the social, Mama packed a basket of food.

"Are we going on a picnic?" Fiddle asked.

Mama laughed. "A picnic in winter?"

Fiddle did not seem to think the weather was too bad. "The sun is out and it's not real cold."

"It's still not picnic weather," Mama said. "We're going into town early, to visit with Granny Buckskin before we go to the social. We'll have lunch at her place."

Fiddle clapped her hands. "Oh, goody!"

But Desty remembered it was Saturday. "Blue Wing won't be at Granny's today. She'll be staying with her mother."

The day was lovely and Champ fairly flew across the prairie with the heavily laden wagon.

On the way, Papa pointed out the new pine school building. The whole building was not very big, Desty thought, but it *was* a school. Over the doorway, a sign read: Thomas Jefferson School.

They stopped and looked in through a window. It was just one big room. The desks were secondhand and some of their tops were scarred by the carvings of pocket knives. Some of them had only empty holes where the little glass inkwells should be. There was a platform running across the front of the room on which was perched a large teacher's desk. On one side of the room stood a big, round stove, its bottom resting on a sheet of tin.

When they reached Granny's, the girls had a delightful surprise. Blue Wing had stayed with Granny, and her mother would stop by to take her to the registration. The rule was that children should have their parents along, if possible, when they registered for school.

Papa suggested he and the boys take a walk. He said they might stop by Bingle's store and see how things were going. Also, he said, they were sure to meet some menfolk who might know about some work Papa might get.

Jason was grouching about school. He wanted to know why he had to go to school if he was old enough to walk and talk with Papa and Burt and other menfolk. Papa put a quick end to his complaint by saying that if Jason did not wish to take a walk, he might sit with Mama at Granny's place. Jason went along with Papa without another word.

Blue Wing was happy to see Desty and Fiddle. "I saw the Abernathys' puppies last week," she told them.

"Oh, could we see them?" Fiddle asked.

"Maybe." Blue Wing mentioned it to Granny.

Granny thought for a moment. "Well, be careful. If you see anyone coming out of the house, you leave right away. You don't want to get your mother in trouble, you know."

Again, Desty felt a great dislike for the Abernathys.

Leaving Granny's, they crossed the street and went behind the buildings. Then quietly they walked north until they came to the back of the big Abernathy house at the end of the street. They looked through the cracks between the high boards of the fence. At first all they could see was the big Dalmation mother dog lying in front of the kennel.

"The little ones are inside," Blue Wing told them.

"Do you think they'll come out?" Desty whispered.

Before Blue Wing could answer, the back door of the house opened and two boys came bounding out. "Come on, Theodore," the tallest one called. "Let's play catch." They began throwing a ball about.

A moment or two later, a little girl followed them. She was all bundled up, but her long, blond curls hung over her muffler and bounced up and down as he ran.

"Let's play hide-and-seek, so I can play too," she pleaded.

The tallest boy scowled at her. "No, not this time, Tildie. Theodore and I want to play ball for a while." The little girl went over to the dog. She petted its head, and it wagged its tail so hard, its whole hindquarters swayed slowly to and fro. Then the girl reached into the kennel and took out one of the younger dogs.

"That's not a puppy," Fiddle began, "it's almost a big dog."

"Sh-h," Desty warned.

At the sound of the girls' voices, the tallest boy looked around quickly. "Somebody's out back," he said and raced for the gate in the fence.

Blue Wing turned and dashed away behind the buildings to the end of the block. Desty grabbed Fiddle's arm and they both leaned hard against the gate. The boy pushed so vigorously on the other side, they had to dig their heels into the ground, to keep the gate from being flung open.

When Desty saw Blue Wing's figure vanish around the corner of the last building she stepped aside, pulling Fiddle with her.

The tall boy pushed through so swiftly, he nearly pitched himself headfirst to the ground. His brother and sister followed him.

"Who are you?" the tall boy asked rudely. Then before they could answer, he said, "I thought it was that Indian kid who tries to hang around here sometimes."

All the while he spoke he surveyed Desty and Fiddle as though making up his mind whether or not they were good enough for him.

"What Indian kid?" Desty asked, trying to look surprised, and hoping Fiddle would not say anything. "We were looking at your dog between the fence boards." She backed off, and tugged at Fiddle's sleeve. "We better be going."

They ran all the way back to Granny's. Blue Wing was waiting outside for them. Her eyes were still wide and frightened.

"They didn't see you," Desty told her and a look of relief came over Blue Wing's face.

Inside Granny and Mama had set the table for lunch.

Shortly afterwards Papa and the boys came back.

"You should see the dining hall. It's so new it was never used before," Jason announced. He did not look grouchy anymore. "It's all ready for the shindig. There's going to be square dancing." He hooked his arm in Burt's and tried to twirl him around, but Burt shoved him away.

It was about two o'clock when they left for the hall. Granny went with them. Blue Wing waited at the laundry and would come later with her mother.

Everyone was invited, even though most of the town children would be going to the other school east of the town.

At a table on one side of the hall sat the teacher for the Thomas Jefferson school. She was a little wispy lady with mouse-colored hair drawn tightly to the back of her head. Dainty gold-rimmed glasses set lightly on the bridge of her thin, straight nose. In front of her on the table was a copy book, into which she was writing the names of her future pupils as they and their parents stood before her.

There were benches and chairs arranged in rows at the back of the hall. Judging by the crowd that filled them, everybody in town must be there.

Mama walked toward the teacher, with Desty on one side and Fiddle on the other. Behind them, Jason shuffled along with his head lowered. Desty glanced back at him and thought that he looked much smaller than usual — he must have been trying to shrink himself.

In front of them in line, a big boy slouched along in worn-out clothes that looked too small for him. With his hands in his pockets, he told the teacher his name, Ben

Matthews. A man with him said he was Ben's father. When his father stated that Ben was thirteen, Ben grinned, sort of sickly. No wonder — he was as tall as Burt!

Ben joined a group of boys in the back of the hall, but his father left immediately.

After Mama had given Desty's name and Fiddle's, they went to the back of the hall, too. But where was Blue Wing? Almost everyone was registered. The teacher wrote the name of the last one in line. Then she closed her copy book and stood up.

When Mr. Stacy, who owned the new hotel, announced that there would be refreshments for all, Desty really became alarmed. If Blue Wing didn't register, would she be allowed to come to school?

As Mr. Stacy spoke, several men set up two long tables along the wall, and some ladies brought out platters of white bread and meat for sandwiches, and bowls of cookies, plus large pitchers of sweet cider. All this, Mr. Stacy said, was provided through the goodness of heart of the Abernathy family. Mr. and Mrs. Abernathy stood up and bowed stiffly while everyone clapped.

"The goodness of heart," Jason whispered, "and the jingle of their pocketbooks."

Mama said sh-h, but Papa and Burt grinned widely.

Oh, where was Blue Wing? Desty hoped with all her heart that Blue Wing's mother didn't change her mind about Blue Wing and school.

Mr. Stacy held up his hand to quiet the loud chatter which swept through the hall at the sight of the food. "You all may feel free to partake of the refreshments, but first I would like to formally introduce the new teacher of Jefferson School to you. She has just come from Missouri, but we hope she won't stay a stranger long. Miss Starks." He shook hands with her as she came to the front of the hall.

Standing beside Mr. Stacy's bulky figure, Miss Starks looked smaller than ever. She seemed completely overwhelmed by the cheers and hand clapping. She smiled a tight little smile, which vanished quickly as though she suddenly thought there was nothing to smile at. She cleared her throat and spoke in a high, nervous voice.

"Ladies and gentlemen, I thank you for your kind welcome. I am happy for my appointment—" she cleared her throat again and shifted her look left and right, "as teacher in your new school. I shall do my best to teach your boys and girls and help them in any way I can. I— I thank you."

Desty heard a snicker behind her. It was Ben Matthews.

"Bet that old crow don't know much more than we do," he whispered loudly. Several boys nearby laughed. She was glad Burt and Jason did not. She wouldn't want to be in Miss Starks' shoes for anything, not with boys like Ben attending the new school.

Miss Starks sat down and Mr. Stacy was speaking again. "We are going to have a square dance, and I hope you all will enjoy — oh, we'll have to wait a moment. I think you have a few more pupils to register, Miss Starks."

Stretching her neck, Desty saw a woman in a limp sunbonnet shuffle towards the teacher. It was Emerson's mother. Emerson followed with his head bowed as though he were going to the hanging tree.

"It's Emmy," Fiddle whispered.

"Sh-h," Mama said.

Then through the door, at last, came Blue Wing and her mother.

As Blue Wing went up to Miss Starks, Ben Matthews stood up and shouted, "I'm not going to school with any old Indian."

There was a dead silence for a moment. So that was what Blue Wing meant about being allowed to attend school. What if there were enough folks against Indians that they could prevent her from coming? Desty couldn't bear the thought of that. Before she knew what she was doing, she stood up and called loudly, "If Blue Wing can't go to school, I won't go either."

Suddenly Fiddle was on her feet. "Hurray for Desty," she shouted.

Then she saw Emerson standing and pointing in her direction. "Hurray for her!"

Desty realized he did not know their names.

Then Fiddle shouted again, "Good old Emmy!"

By this time Mama, her face red and embarrassed, yanked both Desty and Fiddle down to the bench. "Please stop shouting," she ordered.

At that same moment Emerson's mother pulled him down out of view.

Mr. Stacy came to stand beside Miss Starks. "You may take the little girl's name. She *shall* be attending your classes." He looked meaningfully at Ben. Not one more word was said about Blue Wing going to school.

Desty looked anxiously at Mama and then waved to Blue Wing to come sit with them. Blue Wing's mother walked straight toward the door as though there was not one person in the hall. Blue Wing ran to Desty and whispered that she had to go home right away, but that she would see her in school. Then she left as quietly and swiftly as her mother did. Everyone moved towards the tables of food, and ate with relish. Afterward some left, but most stayed, talking in groups.

Mr. Stacy was speaking again. "As I said, after you've all helped yourselves to refreshments, we'll have a square dance. Miss Starks knows the sets well, and she has kindly offered to teach any youngsters who want to dance. They will stay on one side of the floor, however, so as not to interfere with the adults."

Ben slapped his thigh. "Yippee! I know them square dance sets. Let's dance, Harvey." He grabbed a shorter boy and whirled around, stomping his feet awkwardly. His tight pants made his legs look longer and his steps more clumsy. Just like a giant grasshopper, Desty thought, as she watched him jumping around.

Miss Starks tried three times before she caught his sleeve. "You'll have to wait until we're ready. Just stand over there." When she was satisfied that he would stand to one side, she looked over the other children. "Now who else would like to dance? We need three more couples."

There was a lot of giggling and jostling. Desty saw Burt and Jason move away quickly towards Mama and Papa and the other grown-ups. Two girls said they would dance together, but they wouldn't dance with boys. Theodore Abernathy came forward with his sister, Tildie.

Desty secretly felt glad that the Abernathys would

probably attend the other school, east of town.

"Just one more couple," Miss Starks was saying. "How about you?" She looked at Emerson.

Emerson laughed and acted silly. "I don't have no girl."

Holding his arm, Miss Starks again looked over the other children. Four girls ran right out through the door. She came toward Desty and Fiddle. Oh, my goodness, Desty thought, I could never dance in front of all these people. She shrank back, and was ready to grab Fiddle's arm and run, when Fiddle said, "All right, I'll dance with Emmy."

"No, you don't, not when you call me that name." Emerson's eyes looked hurt, but his chin was jutting out bravely.

"I'm sorry," Fiddle said. "I'll call you Em."

"All right, I guess if you can't manage my whole name, Em will do."

Miss Starks arranged them all in their correct places and they could hear the fiddler tuning up. He was ready to play.

"Now this won't be hard if you follow directions," Miss Starks said. "We will let Ben and his partner lead because Ben is tall and you can all see him better."

Ben stuck his chest out so far, Desty feared his worn-out shirt would burst off him.

Then while the fiddler played and the caller called, Miss Starks directed each couple through the steps and positions. Working with just boys and girls, she did not seem nearly so nervous.

Emerson and Fiddle were the last couple in the set.

When it came time to "swing your partner" in the middle of the ring made by the other six dancers, Emerson swung too hard and too fast. Around and around he and Fiddle went.

"I'm getting dizzy," he yelled. His hair was standing straight out from his head.

"Go slower, Emerson," Miss Starks called to him. "Go slower."

But Emerson's head was lowered and he was losing his balance.

"Let go," Fiddle yelled, "let go." Finally she pulled loose.

But Emerson couldn't stop. He went circling wildly by himself, out of the ring of dancers and across the floor, until he flew headfirst into the wall.

He let out a howl that stopped all the dancers and the music and the calling. His mother shuffled as fast as she could to him. One lady ran forward with a glass of cider, and between sniffles, Emerson gulped it down. Then his mother wiped his eyes with her apron, and giving Fiddle a "you again" look, she guided him toward the door.

After the disturbance died down, Mr. Stacey announced that they would go on with the dancing. Desty and Fiddle went back for more cookies. Miss Starks gave up teaching the children to dance. Desty guessed she had had enough with Ben and Emerson in one set.

But the social ended with everyone claiming they had a wonderful time. Even Mama, though Desty didn't see how, since Mama had so many anxious moments with her and Fiddle.

On the way home, Desty told herself that now she was

sure she did not want to move away from the Cherokee Strip.

She was going to mention it to Fiddle when she saw Fiddle pressing her handkerchief over her mouth to muffle her giggling.

"What's so funny?" Jason asked.

"I can't stop thinking how Emmy looked flying around," Fiddle said.

Desty had to grin too, remembering, but she felt that from now on, Emerson would become a better and better friend.

# Chapter
## Twenty-One
# *Home in the*
# *Cherokee Strip*

The following Monday, Desty and Fiddle and Jason had to start classes at the new Jefferson School.

As Papa was getting ready to take them there in the wagon, he mentioned the mess Bingle's store was in when he saw it on Saturday. "It's worse than ever since his son-in-law has been trying to manage it. I might get a day's work helping to straighten it out again."

He told Mama not to worry if he was late coming home. Desty hoped Papa would find work again. If he did, he would be able to buy more materials for their new house. Then Mama might send to Aunt Bessie for her linens and china, and they would be sure of staying in the Strip.

When Papa left them at the school door, he said, "Now mind you, Jason, you get home right after school lets out. You too, girls, there'll be lots of chores to do. I'll be in town and Mama and Burt will have enough work during the day. So no loitering." He grinned at them, clucked his tongue to Champ, and drove off.

In a few minutes, Miss Starks came out and rang a big bell. Everybody pushed through the door into school. Desty and Fiddle shared a double desk on the girls' side of the room. Right behind them, Blue Wing sat beside a big, plump blond girl with a Norwegian name which they could not pronounce.

When they were settled, Desty peeked around at the other students. Some of them had all new clothes, but most of them were like herself and Fiddle. She and Fiddle were wearing the dresses Granny Buckskin made for them at Christmastime. But they had grown in that short time, and already Mama had to let down the hems a little.

Their shoes were uncomfortable though. Too bad, Desty thought, there were no hems in shoes to let out. If the weather were warmer, they could walk home barefoot. But Mama said that they would get new shoes as soon as she and Papa could manage it.

Desty did not care. It was wonderful to go to school again. Books and pencils and paper. They had such a wonderful smell of ink and wood. And she liked Miss Starks very much. The big boys scared her though, with their rough ways. She was glad Jason was in school with them.

At lunch time, Blue Wing ate with them. After they had finished the slabs of corn bread and butter and shared the jar of milk Mama had sent with them, they went outside to play. The first thing they saw was Emerson racing towards them, just a step or two ahead of Ben Matthews.

"You little rat," Ben was yelling, "I'll skin you alive, that's what I'll do."

Emerson darted behind the girls. Just then Jason came up behind Ben. "What's wrong with you, Ben, chasing a little fellow like that?"

Ben, almost a head taller than Jason, turned around. "He was calling names, that's what that little rat was doing."

"I didn't mean you," Emerson said. "I wasn't calling you no names."

Jason laughed. "I wouldn't call you names either," he told Ben. That must have made Ben feel good, because he laughed, too.

Then looking at Blue Wing, he said, "So they do let Indians come here to school."

"You let her alone," Desty said quickly, scarcely thinking of what she was doing. Fiddle stood in front of Blue Wing.

Emerson popped out in full view and yelled at Ben. "Yeah, let her alone. She's a girl." Ben made a jump towards him, and he ducked back again. Ben laughed loudly and turned away. Desty wished with all her might that Ben would quit school.

When they reached home after classes, Desty thought she would never get through telling Mama everything that happened. Fiddle joined in once in a while too. "Yes, and that Emmy, he's still calling names."

"But," Desty said, "I think he'd like for him and us to be good friends." Emerson had stuck up for Blue Wing. For that alone she could like him.

Dusk had come before Papa returned. He came into

the soddy whistling "Blue Tail Fly." That was a good sign. Papa must have had a good day.

Sitting down to supper, he chuckled. "You should see that store. It's a mess. Bingle is so disgusted, he said he better sell out before his son-in-law ruins all the merchandise, the clumsy oaf. I had to work all day to straighten out one side of the place."

Then Papa added, very soberly, "Bingle spoke again about letting me buy the store."

Oh, if Papa only could buy the store, they would be sure of living permanently in the Strip!

But days and weeks passed without Papa saying any more about it. Every other day or so, he went in to work for Bingle, to help out, he said. But he did not buy any more lumber or build any more of their house.

Desty liked school better and better, and Fiddle and Jason did not grumble so much about attending. Still there hung over every day an uncertain feeling. Would she be going here to school next year? Or would they have to leave the Strip?

February passed and so did March. Mama had never sent for her good linens or china, and she had never hung up her windchime. The cottonwoods leafed out on the creek bank, the grass grew green again, and Mama's flowers began to peep through the reddish earth of the little bed alongside the vegetable garden. The clear, clean air swished across the prairie making everything seem new and ready for life. The birds sang loudly and sweetly as if they were trying to shout that spring was here.

It was time Papa plowed his fields and planted his crops. Desty hoped every day that he would start.

Then one evening he came home again whistling "Blue

Tail Fly." With her breath almost stopping, Desty listened to him say, "Well, Bingle has finally settled the question. He is selling his store and he'll let me have it. He and his daughter and son-in-law are going back to Wichita."

Papa took a deep breath. "We'll be paying it off for quite a while, but it will be our own place of business."

Oh, how tall Papa looked, how important he would be, Desty thought.

She wished he would tell them more about it, but Mama poured a cup of coffee for him.

Papa drank all of it before he continued. "On Saturday, we are going to sign the papers. So if the weather is nice, why can't we all go to town for the day."

The weather *was* nice. It must have been the nicest day since the land rush — blue sky, warm sunshine, fresh breezes, bird songs!

Burt seemed especially happy today. Desty knew it was because he would like working in the store. He had probably worried all along that Papa might not get a chance to buy it. Jason, however, said he would rather work the land on the claim.

Going to Barryville was still a wonderful thrill for Desty. Drawing near to the town, they could see the smoke from its chimneys and hear the anvil in the blacksmith's shop.

Desty remembered all the important buildings on the main street, the printing shop, the livery stable near the place where Papa had hoped to have one, the shabby little house with the warped front that held the only "Doctor" sign in town, and the Paradise Ice Cream Parlor. Then there was the furniture store, a clothing shop and of course Mr. Stacy's big new hotel.

Mama and Desty and Fiddle went to Granny's place while Papa and the boys went to see Mr. Bingle. Blue Wing was delighted with their news about the store.

After today, Desty hoped she would not have to worry about leaving the Strip.

At noontime, Papa and the boys came to Granny's for lunch. Papa said that Mr. Bingle had acted as if he were cutting off his right arm when he signed the paper saying that the store henceforth would belong to Papa.

"He hated to part with it, yet he hated to own it when business was bad. He could have put a little more effort in it, though. So could that son-in-law, the —" Papa, Desty knew, was about to say "clumsy oaf" but Mama held up her hand.

Instead Papa laughed happily. "I ordered a sign from Jake Arnold down at the print shop. As soon as you young ladies are through with lunch, I'll give you the privilege of getting it and bringing it to the store."

Blue Wing went with them. They stopped and looked into all the shop windows along the way. In the printing shop, the smell of ink and paint was strong, but Desty liked it. Both ink and paint were used for making words. She liked words, in books, or papers, — but especially on Papa's sign!

It wasn't a very big sign, though, just about a yard long and a foot wide. It read:

### GENERAL STORE
Henry Shawn, Proprietor

Desty was not exactly sure of the meaning of the last word, but it must be something like owner.

"Isn't it wonderful!" Fiddle exclaimed when they were outside once more. She was hugging the sign and insisted on carrying it. "Our own store! I hope Papa lets us have candy whenever we want it, and new dress goods and fancy hair ribbons, and oh, just everything."

Fiddle's eyes were sparkling with joy, but Desty reminded her that Papa had bought the store to make a living for the family. "If we take anything we want, Papa won't make any money."

For a moment Fiddle's face sobered, and then broke again into a flyaway smile. "Oh, we could coax him sometimes."

Desty grinned. Fiddle could never be serious. Then Desty saw Blue Wing smile, too, and slipped her arm in hers. "I hope you're as happy as we are, Blue Wing."

Blue Wing's face straightened as she answered. "Oh, I am. I'm always happy with you and Fiddle. Fiddle makes me happy outside, so I laugh. You make happy inside, so I am not sad even when I don't laugh."

When they reached the store, Mama and Papa and the boys and Granny were there waiting for them.

Papa took the sign and hung it on two hooks over the front door. Then he stood back to survey it, running his hand through his bushy, black hair. His eyes were shining with joy.

"Now we have our business. And we have our land. Soon we'll have our new house, too." He slipped his arm around Mama, giving her a little hug. "Making the Run turned out all right."

The only time Papa's smile disappeared was when Mr. Bingle came out the door for the last time. He picked up the old sign with his name on it which Papa had leaned against the wall, and tucked it under his arm.

When they shook hands, Papa said, "I sure wish you

all the luck in the world when you get back to Wichita."

"Thanks, I wish you the same here. Guess I wasn't cut out to be a storekeeper."

Papa patted his shoulder and said cheerfully, "Don't worry about that, neither was Abe Lincoln."

He took Mr. Bingle's carpetbag and walked with him to the railroad depot where Mr. Bingle's daughter and son-in-law would be waiting for him.

Supper, that evening, was going to be a real celebration in the Shawn soddy. Desty was not surprised about that, but somehow she felt that a celebration would be more in order if everything was absolutely settled about staying for good in the Cherokee Strip. Oh, Papa had his dream of owning a business come true, but what if something happened, and the store failed? Was Mama still thinking of going back to their old home if things went wrong.

However, Mama hummed happily all the while she prepared supper. That was a good sign. Desty looked at her. "Mama, you look as if you had a secret."

"Well, I do — sort of. Papa and I have decided on something, but — well, we'll both tell you after supper."

When Fiddle heard there was another secret to be told, she grew more excited than she had been all day. She kept hurrying Desty through their tasks until supper was ready. And she gulped down her meal so fast, Desty wondered if she even tasted the food.

When they all said they were as full as could be, Mama began clearing the table immediately. Fiddle again worked as fast as she could, breaking a plate while doing so.

"Oh my," Mama said, but instead of scolding, she laughed. "Well, we don't have to worry about one plate any more."

That sounded a little odd, but it must be part of the secret, Desty thought.

Then Mama made her announcement. "I am going to write a letter to Aunt Bessie and Uncle Luke." Desty felt a little disappointed. That wasn't much news; Mama often wrote letters back home. "But," Mama went on, "this time, I'm going to ask Aunt Bessie to send our good linens and china and silverware."

Desty felt a tightness in her chest and a burning behind her eyes. At last Mama was going to send for the things she always said belonged in a permanent home. Her greatest wish had come true.

Mama looked from one to the other as they made delighted remarks, but Desty could only sigh. And even though she couldn't say anything, she was sure Mama knew how she felt.

"Now for the other surprise," Mama continued. Desty felt she could not stand another surprise. "Papa and I have decided," Mama said, "to ask Aunt Bessie and Uncle Luke to consider coming to Oklahoma to homestead. Papa feels sure they can get possession of the Jardine claim. Until then, they can build a soddy on our claim."

While everyone said "Golly," "Aunt Bessie," "Gee," Mama turned to look at Papa.

Papa nodded happily. "Yes, and meanwhile Uncle Luke can help us put in our crop. It will be a pleasure now that we don't have to depend only on it to live."

Desty knew Papa was thinking of their store again. He set a stool against the sod wall, sat down, leaned back and put his feet up on another stool in front of him.

Meanwhile Mama had gotten two pieces of paper and was settling herself on the bench at the table. "While I'm writing to Aunt Bessie, you children can each write a short note on this other paper and I will send it with my letter."

As all hands reached for it, Mama held it aloft. "Burt's first, he's the oldest."

After Burt and Jason labored over a few words mostly to Uncle Luke, since they felt boys should write to men, the paper was passed to the girls.

"You go first, Fiddle." Desty offered.

Finally, when Desty's turn came, she knew just what she wanted to write.

> Dear Aunt Bessie:
>
> Please come. All Oklahoma needs to make it the best place in the world is you — and Uncle Luke.
>
> > Love,
> > Adeste Marie.

She signed her full name as Mama had taught her to even before she ever went to school. Her eyes felt burn–y again, and she blinked. Aunt Bessie and Uncle Luke would be like extra anchors to hold the Shawns in Oklahoma.

When the letters were done, Jason said. "Let's sing some songs."

Papa, lighting his pipe, said he would enjoy that. "But first," he told Jason, "bring me the box with my house slippers."

And for the first time in her life, Desty saw Papa take off his shoes and put on house slippers. He was settled now in his mind, she thought. He didn't have the feeling that he would have to be ready to go off somewhere.

The evening went far too quickly. Desty wanted it to last forever. "Peaceful" was the only word she could think of for the way she felt now. She would not have to worry any more about the way things would turn out.

But soon Mama was saying, "Time for bed."

As usual after a wonderful, exciting time, Desty could not fall asleep, hard as she tried. An hour slid by. She could hear Mama and Papa leaving the kitchen for bed. She knew Fiddle was asleep. She was sure the boys were too. Later, she could even hear Papa snore, yet she was still wide awake.

Over and over she kept thinking, we are going to stay in the Cherokee Strip, we're going to stay!

Then she slid out of bed, opened her treasure box quietly and took from it the little bag of Kansas earth. Tip-toeing from the bedroom, she stole through the doorway out into the night. Then opening the bag, she let the dry earth sift down onto the red Oklahoma clay. She did not need it any more, this was home to the Shawns from now on.

She sighed, and smiled as her hair was stirred by the soft, cool breeze. The night was beautiful. The big, round moon hung high in the Oklahoma sky and the stars twinkled so brightly they seemed to be swinging in the air. Desty almost expected them to tinkle like a windchime.